How God Used A Drought And An

UMBRELLA
And Other Devotional Stories

Joel R. Beeke & Diana Kleyn
Illustrated by Jeff Anderson

CHRISTIAN FOCUS PUBLICATIONS

© copyright 2003 Reformation Heritage Books
Published by Christian Focus Publications
and Reformation Heritage Books
ISBN: 1-85792-818-0
Christian Focus Publications Ltd,
Geanies House, Fearn, Tain,
Ross-shire, IV20 1TW.
Scotland, Great Britain
www.christianfocus.com
email: info@christianfocus.com
Reformation Heritage Books
2919 Leonard St, NE, Grand Rapids, MI, 49525
Phone: 616-977-0599
Fax: 616-285-3246
email: orders@heritagebooks.org
Website: www.heritagebooks.org
Illustrations and Cover illustration by Jeff Anderson
Cover design by Alister Macinnes
Printed and bound in Great Britain by
Cox & Wyman

Building on the Rock - Book titles and Themes
Book 1: How God Used a Thunderstorm
Living for God and The Value of Scripture
Book 2: How God Stopped the Pirates
Missionary Tales and Remarkable Conversions
Book 3: How God Used a Snowdrift
Honoring God and Dramatic Deliverances
Book 4: How God Used a Drought and an Umbrella
Faithful Witnesses and Childhood Faith
Book 5: How God Sent a Dog to Save a Family
God's Care and Childhood Faith

Acknowledgements

All of the Christian stories contained in these books are based on true happenings, most of which occurred in the nineteenth century. We have gleaned them from a variety of sources, including several books by Richard Newton, then rewrote them in contemporary language. Many of them are printed here for the first time; others were previously printed, without the accompanying devotional material, in a series titled *Building on the Rock* by the Netherlands Reformed Book and Publishing and by Reformation Heritage Books in the 1980s and 1990s.

Thanksgiving is rendered to God first of all for His help in preparing this series of books. Without Him we can do nothing. We would also like to thank James W. Beeke for supplying some helpful material; Jenny Luteyn, for contributing several of the stories; Jeff Anderson for his illustrations; and Catherine Mackenzie, for her able and invaluable editing. Finally, we would like to thank our loyal spouses, Mary Beeke and Chris Kleyn, for their love, support, and encouragement as we worked on these books over several years. We pray earnestly that the Lord will bless these stories to many hearts.

Joel R. Beeke and Diana Kleyn
Grand Rapids, Michigan

Contents

How to use this book

The stories within this book and the other titles in the *Building on the Rock* series are all stories with a strong gospel and biblical message. They are ideal for more than one purpose.

1. Devotional Stories: These can be used as a child's own personal devotional time or as part of family worship.

Please note that each story has at least one scripture reference. Every story has a scripture reading referred to at the end which can be used as part of the individual's or the family's Bible reading program. Many of the stories have other references to scripture and some have several extra verses which can also be looked up.

Each story has two prayer points at the end of the book. These are written as helps to prayer and are not to be used as prayers themselves. Reading these pointers should help the child or the family to think about issues connected with the story that need prayer in their own life, the life of their church or the world. Out of the two prayer points written for each story, one prayer point is written specifically for those who have saving faith while the other point is written in such a way that both Christians and non-believers will be brought to pray about their sinful nature and perhaps ask God for His salvation or thank Him for His gift of it.

Each story has also a question and discussion section at the end where the message of the story can either be applied to the reader's life or where a direct question is asked regarding the story itself or a related passage of scripture. The answers to the direct questions are given at the end of the book. Scripture references are indexed at the back of the book. Beside each chapter number you will read the scripture references referred to. These include references within the story, question or scripture reading sections.

2. Children's Talks: As well as all the features mentioned above, the following feature has a particular use for all those involved in giving children's talks at Church, Sunday School, Bible Class, etc. At the end of the series in Book 5, you will find a series index of scripture in biblical order where you will be able to research what books in the series have reference to particular Scriptures. The page number where the Scripture appears is also inserted. Again, all Scriptures from stories, question sections, and Scripture readings are referred to in this section

It is also useful to note that each book will have a section where the reader can determine the length of specific stories beforehand. This will sometimes be useful for devotional times but more often will be a useful feature for those developing a children's talk where they are very dependent on the time available.

Shorter Length Stories

The following stories are shorter in length than the average length of story included in this book. They therefore may be used for family devotions, children's talks, etc. where less time is available:

Longer Length Stories

The following stories are longer in length than the average length of story included in this book. They therefore may be used for family devotions, children's talks, etc. where more time is available:

1. The Carpenter's Apprentice

During a revival of religion in a town in eastern Pennsylvania, a carpenter's apprentice named John was one of the first to be converted. He became an earnest Christian, and did much work for God and the church. His great desire was to tell others about the Lord Jesus Christ and their need of Him for their salvation. John had not had much education, and had no money to go to school to be a teacher or a minister, but he did whatever he could, speaking to people and helping others in need.

John's employer was not a Christian, nor was he interested in becoming a Christian. "I am a good man, John," the carpenter said. "I am always honest in my business, and try to help others when I can. I am a good husband and father. I don't need religion, John!"

One evening, John's employer was at a business meeting, and John had gone to a prayer meeting at church. When the apprentice came home, he went to the barn so that he could spend some time alone in prayer before going to bed. He poured out his soul in earnest prayer to God. He prayed aloud, asking God for the conversion of sinners, and for the building up of His kingdom.

While John was praying, the carpenter returned home. He put his horse in the barn, and paused when he heard a voice. It sounded as though someone was in distress. As he climbed up the ladder to the loft, he discovered John on his knees, interceding for him! Why would John pray so earnestly for him? Curious, he stayed to listen. It seemed John was even weeping on his behalf! He begged the Lord to have mercy on his employer and to make him a Christian. With earnest and loving words he entreated the Friend of sinners to visit his dear employer, and prayed the Holy Spirit to awaken him from the sleep of death and show him that he needed something more than outward goodness to rest upon.

The carpenter was amazed. Did John really care that much? Then he began to wonder if perhaps John was right. Was his good lifestyle enough to satisfy God?

God made that prayer the means of the carpenter's awakening. His conscience began to speak. The Holy Spirit showed him sins he didn't realize were sins. No longer was he an innocent man of good deeds. He was a guilty sinner!

That night he could not sleep. The more he thought, the more he realized how great his sins were. But God did not forsake this poor carpenter. With tears of repentance, the carpenter asked God for forgiveness, remembering how tenderly John had spoken of his beloved Redeemer, the crucified Savior of sinners. Through the work of the Holy Spirit, the carpenter was given to believe in the Lord Jesus Christ alone, and rejoiced in the forgiveness of his sins. He felt like a criminal set free. "I'm free!" he exclaimed with happy tears.

John and his employer rejoiced together and thanked the Lord for His merciful kindness. The two men remained close friends, and did much work in God's kingdom out of thankfulness for such undeserved grace.

Question: What will God do if we confess our sins to Him in truth?
Scripture Reading: 1 John 1.

2. A Poor Man Made Rich

Joseph was a young man who lived in London, England. Because he'd had an accident as a child he found it hard to think clearly and some things were just too difficult for him to cope with. His life had not been easy. As a boy, he had often been teased. Now that he was older, he lived alone and had no friends. He was poor. He made a little money by running errands and carrying packages for people.

One Sunday Joseph was carrying a large bundle of yarn on his back. He had to deliver it to someone on the other side of the city. He never had been taught not to work on Sunday. In fact, Joseph had been taught nothing about God. So, when he passed a church and heard singing, he was curious and went inside. It was a church where one of the old Puritans was pastor. The people were neatly dressed, and a few turned to stare at Joseph in his rags.

The minister read his text from 1 Timothy 1:15: "This is a faithful saying, and worthy of all acceptation, that Christ Jesus came into the world to save sinners; of whom I am chief." Very simply and clearly, the pastor preached about this faithful saying; that there is eternal salvation for the worst sinner only through the worthiness of Jesus Christ, the God who made all things.

This wonderful message did not seem to impress the congregation, but Joseph never took his eyes off the minister. He eagerly listened to every word. When the service ended, Joseph left quietly. He talked softly to himself as he walked: "I've never heard this before. Jesus Christ, the God who made all things, came into the world to save sinners like Joseph. And this is true. And it is a faithful saying."

The people who heard Joseph were embarrassed; they left him alone. They thought he was a very strange man.

Not long after this Joseph became ill, with a high fever. As the fever raged, he tossed on his bed and repeated over and over, "Joseph is the chief of sinners. But Jesus Christ came into the world to save sinners, and Joseph loves Him for this."

His landlady did her best to care for Joseph, and when she heard him talking, she called a religious neighbor to visit him. The neighbor tried to calm Joseph by telling him he was a good man.

"No! No!" answered Joseph. "Joseph is not good! Joseph is the chief of sinners; but this is a faithful saying that Jesus, who made all things, came to save sinners. Why may not Joseph be saved after all?"

The neighbor was confused by this kind of talk. But he was a kind-hearted man, and wanted to help. After questioning Joseph about the pastor and the church, the man looked for the pastor and asked him to please visit Joseph.

A few days later the pastor came to see Joseph. Joseph had not been getting better, but rather, worse every day. He was now very weak, so weak that he had not talked for some time.

"Joseph," called the landlady softly. "The pastor is here."

But Joseph seemed to be asleep.

"Joseph," said the minister.

Joseph's eyes flew open in surprise when he recognized the pastor's voice. He struggled to sit up, but he was too weak and fell back on the pillow. Clasping the minister's hand, he cried in a feeble, trembling voice, "Oh, sir! You are the friend of the Lord Jesus! You spoke so well of Him! Joseph is the chief of sinners, but it is a faithful saying that Jesus Christ, the God who made all things, came into the world to save sinners. And why not Joseph? Oh, pray to that Jesus for me! Pray that He may save me! Tell Him that Joseph thinks he loves Him for coming into the world to save sinners like Joseph."

The minister was amazed. He had been asked to visit a confused man, but this was no confused man! This was God's work. With joy in his heart, the minister prayed earnestly for Joseph. When he finished, Joseph thanked him most sincerely. Then he put his hand under his pillow and took out an old rag in which was tied a little bit of money. He placed it in the pastor's hands and said, "Joseph in his foolishness, was keeping this money for his old age, but Joseph will never be old. Take it and give it to the poor friends of Jesus. Tell them that Joseph gave it to them for His sake who came into the world to save sinners, of whom Joseph is chief."

When Joseph had finished speaking, he seemed to suddenly fall asleep. The strain of talking had been too much for him. Quietly, the pastor sat by Joseph's side. A few moments later Joseph died.

With tears running down his cheeks, the faithful minister left the room. They were tears of joy and thankfulness at the simple faith God had worked in this young man. He often told this story of poor Joseph who had been made rich, and who said with the apostle Paul, "This is a faithful saying, and worthy of all acceptation, that Christ Jesus came into the world to save sinners; of whom I am chief."

Question: Who did Jesus come to the world to save?
Scripture reading: Matthew 11:25-30.

3. A Real Friend

L

Jane Clark was an orphan who lived with her grandmother in a little village in England. Mrs. Clark was a God-fearing woman, and did her best to teach Jane the truths of God's Word.

The pastor of the village, Rev. North, loved children. Every Sunday, he and his daughter would visit all the classes in the Sunday School and reward those children who showed good behavior and attention. Often Miss North would bring several books to give to some children who had learned all their memory verses, or who had attended faithfully.

On this particular Sunday, Jane received a book for knowing all her memory verses. She was so happy with her new book! Grandmother did not have extra money to buy books. Jane thanked Miss North with a bright smile and a hug.

As she was returning home, however, a dirty, ragged girl ran up to her and grabbed the book from her hand. Jane knew who this girl was: Lucy Jackson. She was the oldest child of a carpenter who lived not far from Jane and her grandmother. Tom Jackson, Lucy's father, could hardly ever get work, because everyone knew he liked to spend most of his time at the tavern. So, Tom spent most of his time at home, and his wife became so discouraged by all this, that she neglected her household and began drinking too. The result was that Lucy had never been taught how to read or to work, nor was she taught what was right and wrong.

Jane begged Lucy to give back the beautiful book, but Lucy ignored her.

"You're ripping the pages!" cried Jane. "It's a brand new book!"

"I just want to look at the pictures," answered Lucy. She paged through the book, then threw it on the ground. "Here. Have your book back. I don't like it anyway."

Jane bent down to pick up the book. She was crying. Jane was not only crying because Lucy had torn her book, but because she was so ragged and rude. When Lucy and Jane were very small children, they used to play together often, but lately Lucy had become so naughty that Jane did not want to play with her anymore. What had happened to the sweet friend Lucy used to be? She had been so gentle and kind, but not anymore.

"What is the matter, my dear?" asked Grandma when Jane came crying into the house.

"I got a beautiful book from Miss North, and Lucy grabbed it and ripped the pages and threw it in the dirt," sobbed Jane.

Grandma comforted Jane, then said, "The best thing you can do for Lucy is to be kind to her. God, in His great kindness to you, has given you friends, and good clothes, and food, and a happy home. Now you must make yourself useful to those poor people who are not as well off as yourself."

"But we don't have money to buy food and clothes for Lucy and her family," protested Jane.

"Yes, that's true," agreed her grandmother. "But you may be useful in another way. Lucy has no friends to teach her what is right and wrong. Her parents do not send her to church or Sunday School. What if you would teach her what is right, and try to convince her that lying and stealing are sins? Ask the Lord to help you. I know her parents are not home right now, so you could go there now. But Jane, if Lucy does not listen to you, and begins to use bad language, do not stay. Paul says, 'Evil communications corrupt good manners.'" (1 Corinthians 15:33)

Jane smiled. "I'll go and visit Lucy right now, Grandma. I'll tell her about God and the Bible and the way of salvation."

Jane and her grandmother prayed before she left, asking God to help Jane speak to Lucy, and to make Lucy His child.

When Jane arrived at Lucy's house, she found Lucy crying bitterly. When she understood that it was because Lucy wished she had a book, Jane said, "I wish I could give you my book, but it was Miss

North's gift to me, and it would not be right to give away a gift. But I know how you could get your very own book."

"How?" asked Lucy, wiping away her tears.

"You could come with me to the Sunday School. I'll teach you how to behave, and I'll help you with your memory verses, and then you could earn a book too!"

Lucy was not enthusiastic. "I'd be embarrassed to go," she said softly. "I'm almost eight years old, and I don't even know my ABC's, and you can read your Bible already."

"That wouldn't matter at all," answered Jane, "but if it would make you feel better, I could teach you a little."

"I don't have any time for learning," sighed Lucy. "I have to watch my little brothers all day."

"What about when they take their naps? You could study then," persisted Jane. "I'll come every day before school, and I'll teach you to pray and ask our heavenly Father to give you a new heart, and to help you learn to read." Jane paused, then added, "Lucy, did you know that the Bible is God's own Word, and that it says that all liars will be burned in a lake of fire? And people who steal will be punished by God for ever."

Lucy's eyes widened. "Is that really true? Nobody ever told me that before!"

Jane was surprised that Lucy had never heard these things before. "They are written in God's holy book," answered Jane solemnly.

Lucy began to cry. "What will I do then? God must be very angry with me. I've told so many lies, and I've stolen all kinds of things from other people. I've fought with other children and called them awful names!"

"If you are sorry for what you've done, and pray to God to forgive you, and ask the Holy Spirit to make you clean, He will forgive you. God is so merciful and kind that He has sent His Son Jesus Christ to die on the Cross and take the punishment of sinners, so that sinners like we are may be forgiven and go to heaven when they die."

"I am very sorry for what I've done," said Lucy, "and I hope God will forgive me. Nobody ever told me any of this before. We never go to church."

Jane gave Lucy a hug. "I'd love to teach you whatever I know, and sometimes, maybe you could visit us and talk with Grandma. She knows much more than I do. And we will pray for you, that God may forgive you your sins. But I must go now or Grandma will wonder what's keeping me so long."

Jane promised to come back the following day, and then she hurried home. Her grandmother rejoiced to hear how well the conversation had gone, and promised to pray for Lucy.

Jane got up a half hour earlier the next morning so that she would have time to see Lucy before school. She was puzzled when there was no answer to her knock, but she waited a few minutes and knocked again. At last Lucy opened the door, but she looked as though she had just climbed out of bed. "Oh, come in, Jane," she yawned.

Jane looked around and noticed that the house was very dirty and untidy. Lucy's three brothers were crying and asking for their breakfast.

"Where's your mother?" asked Jane.

"She always gets up late. It's my job to take care of my brothers," answered Lucy.

Jane was disappointed. By the time Lucy would have gotten breakfast ready for herself and her three brothers, it would be time for Jane to go to school. "Lucy," said Jane, "if you would get up earlier, we would have time to learn to read, and to learn the memory verses from the Sunday School."

"I don't like getting up early," answered Lucy, "but if you are serious about teaching me, I would not mind at all!"

"I'd love to teach you, Lucy." Jane hesitated, then said gently, "You know, Lucy, if you would always get up early and sweep the floor and wash the dishes and wash and dress your brothers and feed them before I get here we will have a half hour to ourselves. And when your mother gets up, you should try your best to be helpful for her in any way you can. Maybe you could even teach your brothers what I teach you."

"I'll try," answered Lucy, but Jane could tell she felt overwhelmed at all these duties.

"Have you prayed to God this morning, to ask Him to help you?"

"I don't know how to pray," said Lucy.

"Come then," said Jane, "we'll pray together." They knelt together on the dirty floor. "When we pray," continued Jane, "we should try to think about God, and not about playing or other things. God knows what we are thinking, and if we think about things we shouldn't think about, He will be angry with us. But God loves to hear children pray to Him."

Then Jane prayed aloud, asking God to bless Lucy and help her as she learned to read and to learn memory verses. She asked Him to give them both a new heart to love and obey God and walk in His ways.

"Thank you," said Lucy, with tears in her eyes. "I hope God will forgive my wickedness and take away my sins. Do you really think God will listen to me when I pray?"

Jane's eyes filled with tears as well. "Oh yes! God will hear and forgive you for the sake of Jesus Christ. Jesus Himself said, 'Suffer little children to come unto me and forbid them not, for of such is the kingdom of heaven.'"

"Even children like me?" asked Lucy.

"Yes, Lucy," smiled Jane.

As soon as Jane left, Lucy began sweeping the kitchen, making it neat and clean. It made her feel very happy to be useful to her mother. But when Mrs. Jackson came downstairs, she was in a bad mood, and scolded Lucy for all kinds of things for which Lucy was not to blame. Lucy wanted to shout angry words to her mother, but she remembered that God would not be pleased with that, so she did not say anything at all, but meekly served her mother her breakfast.

So the days passed by. Every morning Jane stopped by before school. Lucy would have the boys dressed and fed, and the house looked better every day. Even Lucy's father was pleased to find things looking cleaner and tidier at home.

One Saturday, after about two months, Jane said, "I think you could come with me to Sunday School tomorrow. You can read a little bit now."

"I don't know if my mother would let me," said Lucy. "Who would take care of my little brothers when I am not home?"

"Let's go and see my grandmother. Maybe she has an idea," suggested Jane.

So the two girls, along with Lucy's brothers, walked the short way to Jane's house. When they told Mrs. Clark that Lucy wanted to go to Sunday School, she said, "Jane tells me what a nice girl you have become, Lucy. I will go and ask your mother myself if you can go to Sunday School, and I think your brother, Johnny, is old enough to go too. I will offer to take care of your two youngest brothers while you go. But let me look at your dress. Little girls who go to Sunday School should try to look their best."

"I can wash my dress before I go to bed tonight, Mrs. Clark," replied Lucy eagerly. "And I'll wash Johnny's clothes too!"

"Good. I'm going right now to talk with your mother. I'll be back soon," she smiled.

The children waited impatiently for Mrs. Clark to return. When she did, she said, "Well, Lucy and Johnny, your mother has agreed to let you go, and I will take care of the two little ones."

Lucy almost cried for joy, and thanked Mrs. Clark many times for her kindness.

"You're welcome, dear," answered Mrs. Clark. "Now go home, and show your mother how thankful you are by doing what you can for her."

Lucy did as the old lady told her, and thanked her mother in both words and deeds. Before she went to bed she washed her and her brother's clothes, and also remembered to thank God for the kind friends He had given her.

She awoke very early Sunday morning. She was so excited, and a bit nervous too. Lucy and her brothers arrived at Jane's house right on time. Mrs. Clark welcomed them, and smiled kindly at them. Before the three children left for Sunday School, she admonished them, "Learn all you can. Sit quietly and listen well. After Sunday School, you will go to the church service with Lucy. Now let me explain what the Sabbath is and why we go to God's house."

Lucy, Johnny, and Jane listened carefully as the old woman spoke. "Our good and gracious God has commanded us to lay aside our cares and labors for one day each week. God has told us to gather together in His house on the Sabbath to worship Him. He has promised salvation to poor sinners through Jesus Christ our Lord. When we are in God's house, we do not talk, but we keep our minds on God and on His Word. When we enter the church, we should ask God to bless the message the pastor brings, and to bless the pastor as he brings it. We must ask the Lord to work in our hearts with His Holy Spirit, and make us useful servants in His kingdom."

Lucy and her brother, Johnny, seemed awed by all this, and when Lucy started to say that she didn't dare to go anymore, Mrs. Clark hugged her and suggested that they pray together. After that Lucy felt better, and they set out for Sunday School. Lucy and Johnny asked many questions about God, and Jesus, and the Holy Spirit, and the church. Jane was kept busy trying to answer all the questions, and soon they entered the Sunday School classroom and quickly sat down.

When Miss North came in she welcomed Lucy and Johnny. "I hope you come every week now," she smiled. Miss North knew the Jackson family, as she and her father and mother had visited them several times, trying to persuade them to attend church. She gave Lucy and Johnny a picture book of Bible stories, telling them to read it to their younger brothers. Lucy smiled her thanks, telling Miss North she would take very good care of the book.

When Sunday School and the service were over, the children walked home thoughtfully. Lucy thanked Mrs. Clark for watching her brothers, and the old lady promised to do it again the following Sunday.

Lucy and Johnny showed their parents the new book. Mrs. Jackson paid no attention, but Mr. Jackson was pleased. He had noticed the change in his daughter's behavior, and the effect it had on the boys and the household. When Lucy went to bed that night, she thanked God for the opportunity to go to His house that day and to hear so many wonderful things.

On Wednesday morning, Reverend North visited the Jackson family. Lucy was on an errand, and her brothers were playing outside. The pastor was very honest. "I trust you've noticed the change in your daughter, though I dare say it has not come about because of any effort on your part. I pray, for your souls' sakes and those of your children, that you would think seriously about eternity. It is your duty, as parents, to teach your children the things of God. You must answer to God on the day of judgment for the use of your time and the words that you speak. This is a serious matter. Please think carefully about what you are doing."

Mr. Jackson put his head in his hands. He seemed moved by what the minister said. But Mrs. Jackson was angry.

"I have spoken honestly to you both," persisted the minister. "I do not do this to irritate you, but to lovingly admonish you. Seek God's grace to repent of sin and to believe in Christ. If you love and serve Him, and pray for His forgiveness and grace, and walk in His ways, God will be your friend, and refuge, and shield, and His blessing will rest upon you now and for all eternity."

Mr. Jackson shed tears, but Mrs. Jackson turned her back on the minister. When Reverend North rose to leave, Mr. Jackson followed him to the door, but couldn't speak a word.

"Think about it, Thomas," said Reverend North gently. "I will visit you again soon."

Mr. Jackson went to his workshop, thinking about the words the pastor had spoken. For some time after this, Mr. Jackson did his best to be a better father and husband. But it is a difficult thing to break bad habits, especially when we do not truly seek God's help. So it was not long before Mr. Jackson fell back into his old ways, spending most of his time at the tavern. But, sometimes, when Lucy would beg him not to go, or Reverend North would visit, he would resist temptation and stay home.

As for Lucy's mother, she refused to think about the minister's words, and when Lucy or her father talked about God, it made her furious. Sometimes Lucy's parents had terrible arguments when Mr. Jackson tried to tell his wife she should change her ways, and the children would tremble with fear. Mr. Jackson would be tempted to storm out of the house and go to the tavern, but Lucy would talk to him gently about God and His mercy and how we must ask Him to help us. This would calm him down and awaken his conscience, so that he would not go. Lucy would read to him from the Bible, or some good book that Miss North had given them. In this way, Lucy often kept her father from bad company, and, by the grace of God, put serious thoughts into his mind.

Some time after this, Mrs. Jackson became very ill. Lucy was worried, and begged her mother to allow her to get the doctor. But Mrs. Jackson did not want to hear that her life was in danger. She was afraid of death, so she told herself she would soon be better. At last, after several weeks, Mr. Jackson got the doctor anyway. Mrs. Jackson was in constant pain, which made her impatient and difficult. When the doctor came, he said there was no hope that she would get well again, but that she would not live much longer.

Although Mr. Jackson had known his wife was very ill, he was shocked by the doctor's words. Quickly he went to Reverend North and asked him to pray with his wife. Rev. North came, and talked with Mrs. Jackson about sin and forgiveness and the Lord Jesus Christ.

"No!" said Mrs. Jackson angrily. "Do not talk to me about repentance! It is too late! I cannot hope for mercy. I have been a very wicked sinner. I have neglected my family. God is punishing me with this dreadful sickness. I dare not hope for mercy."

Lucy, hearing her mother speak in this way, wept as if her heart would break.

"Oh, Lucy," cried Mrs. Jackson, "you have no cause for grief. You have taken the right path, and God will be your friend and bless you here and in the world to come. May you never forget the dying state of your wretched mother and learn from that to flee the ways of wickedness which end in eternal death!"

Soon after this, she lost her speech, and seemed determined not to listen to Reverend North's or Lucy's pleadings. She seemed to be greatly troubled. Several days later she died. Was she forgiven in the end? God only knows.

The shocking death of his wife had such an effect on Mr. Jackson that, by God's grace, he became a changed man. He never again went to the tavern. He went regularly to God's house, taught his children about God, and worked hard to support his family. He became a man who walked closely with God, and became an example to those around him.

However, he soon lost his health, and Lucy and her brothers, now teenagers, did what they could to earn money and trusted God to supply all their needs. The Jackson family became much respected in the village as a God-fearing family. It was not uncommon to see Mr. Jackson and his children sitting together in the evening, listening to Lucy as she read a chapter from the Bible or from some good book which someone had lent them. Then they would pray and sing together, and talk of the Lord's gracious work in their hearts and lives.

Jane cared for her grandmother until her death, later becoming a Sunday School teacher. She married a kind, God-fearing man and she and her husband raised their children in God's ways.

Jane and Lucy remained good friends. Lucy never forgot to thank the Lord for Jane, for Jane had been used by the Lord to lead her to Christ.

Question: How did Jane respond to Lucy's initial hurtfulness?
Scripture readings: Exodus 33:7-11; Proverbs 17:7, 18:24 & James 4:4.

4. A Sister's Influence

Eight-year-old Tommy had learned to swear. Whenever he heard bad language, he would treasure it in his mind, and use his new words to shock his neighbors, some of whom were God-fearing.

After some time, a neighbor hearing Tommy swear, decided to talk to Tommy's sister, who was babysitting since the parents were away from home on business. Katie was very sad to hear this about her youngest brother, and talked to him very seriously.

"Don't you listen to the Bible stories I tell you every day, Tommy?" asked Katie sadly. "God is not pleased with your swearing. He will punish you if you do not stop and ask Him for forgiveness. I will have to tell Dad about this, Tommy."

This frightened the little boy. "No! Don't tell Dad! He'll be so angry! Katie, don't tell him, please!"

Tommy cried so hard that Katie felt sorry for him. "I'll tell you what, Tommy. If you promise me never to swear again, I won't tell Dad."

Tommy hesitated. "All right," he agreed reluctantly.

True to his promise, Tommy never swore again. As he grew up, however, he chose friends who swore and behaved badly. Although Tommy joined in their wicked behavior, he never swore.

"Tommy" became "Tom," and, when he was fourteen, Katie had an opportunity to speak to him about the need to be born again. Katie was married by this time, and Tom had come to spend a week with her. She spoke to her brother about the uncertainty of life and that our hearts become harder the longer we refuse Christ. She tried to tell him of the joys of belonging to Jesus Christ, but Tom just laughed.

"Don't talk about that now, Katie! What's the use of bothering with religion now? I'll wait till I'm grown up and settled down. Then I'll decide."

Katie pleaded with her brother, but it was of no use. He laughed at her, and told her it was good enough for her, but he was young and wanted to enjoy life.

At last Katie said, "Well, my dear brother, you know the truth. You have been warned. I pray God it will not have to be said of you, 'Seeing thou hatest instruction, and castest my words behind thee' (Psalm 50:17)." Then she left the room weeping.

Tom walked off whistling a cheery tune, but he could not forget his sister's tears and her warnings so lovingly given. Especially her last words — that text — stuck in his mind.

Two years passed, and although it seemed Tom was continuing his reckless lifestyle, he often thought about his sister's words, and the passage she had quoted from the Psalms. Sometimes he wondered if God would punish him by sudden death, and it frightened him. Then he thought that maybe he should begin to seek the Lord.

Katie did not speak to her brother about the Lord during this time, but she did pray daily for him. So she was surprised when she received a visit from Tom. By now he was sixteen, and had gained the reputation of being a wild young man.

But Katie met a distressed, anxious young man that day. She hardly dared to hope that the Holy Spirit had begun to work in his hard heart. But it was true!

"Katie, I don't know what to do!" Tom burst out. "I can't stop thinking about those words from the Psalms you quoted to me two years ago. I've tried to read in the Bible Mom gave me, but all I read is about judgments for the wicked. And when I read about God's love and mercy, I dare not believe He will be merciful to me after all my rejection of Him!"

Praying inwardly for guidance, Katie talked with her dear brother. She read God's Word and prayed with him, encouraging him to seek God's forgiveness. She pointed out texts that spoke of God's abundant mercy. "For thy mercy is great above the heavens: and thy truth reacheth unto the clouds" (Psalm. 108:4). "Who is a God like unto thee, that pardoneth iniquity, and passeth by the transgression of the remnant of his heritage? he retaineth not his anger for ever, because he delighteth in mercy" (Micah 7:18).

Tom spent several weeks at his sister's home, and used the time to search the Scriptures, pray, and talk with his sister and her husband. The Lord blessed this time, and was pleased to graciously wash away Tom's sins and renew his heart.

Children, don't be afraid to talk to your brothers and sisters about the Lord. It may be that the Lord will use you to influence your brother or sister to turn from sin to God. Ask the Lord to give you and your brothers and sisters a new heart that loves God above all, and your neighbor as yourself.

Question: How did Katie warn her brother? In Philemon verse 6 what is needed for the effectual communication of the gospel? Scripture readings: Matthew 10:19; Luke 21:15 & 2 Corinthians 2:13.

5. An Absent Daughter

Mr. Southerland's daughter Abby had left home. Abby's mother had died when she was only eight years old. Her five brothers and sisters were children of God, as was her father. But Abby, now sixteen, turned a deaf ear to their warnings and pleadings.

Mr. Southerland prayed for Abby every day. It made him so sad that she did not love and serve God. After much prayer, he decided to call his children together to pray especially for Abby. It was a solemn hour. The brothers and sisters prayed earnestly for their dear sister. The father wrestled with God for the salvation of his beloved daughter. They asked the Holy Spirit to work in her heart and turn her from sin to God.

And how was Abby spending her evening? She was far away from her family, and unaware that they were pleading for her conversion. Abby had planned to go to a party with her friends, but since she had caught a cold, she had to stay home. At the very hour that her family was praying for her, she was in bed, reading one of her father's letters. The simple words, "God bless you, my child, and make you a child of the Lord Jesus Christ" struck home like lightning to her soul.

"A child of Jesus!" She knew her father was getting old; soon he would die, and she would have no earthly father. If she could have a heavenly Father, how happy she would be! But how?

"I must pray," she thought.

She knelt by her bed, but was so overwhelmed by the sense of her sins, that for some minutes she could think of nothing to say. At last she cried, "God, be merciful to me a sinner!" (Luke 18:13)

The family's prayer of faith, and Abby's broken cry for pardon, went up together to the throne of God. Four days later, a letter was handed to Mr. Southerland by his granddaughter.

"Who is it from?" he asked, for the old man was nearly blind.

"It's from Aunt Abby," replied the little girl.

"Abby, my dear child!" he exclaimed.

Opening the letter with a trembling hand, he called to his daughter to come and read it to him.

The first words Abby had written were, "Dear father, God has saved my soul."

"Praise God!" exclaimed Mr. Southerland. "Blessed be His holy name! The Lord's promises are true; the Lord is faithful. 'Now lettest thou thy servant depart in peace, according to thy word, for mine eyes have seen thy salvation' (Luke 2:29-30). God has fulfilled his promise, 'And it shall come to pass, that before they call, I will answer; and while they are yet speaking, I will hear' (Isaiah 65:24)."

Abby came home and spent a few blessed years with her dear father before he died. God was Abby's Father in heaven, so she was not lonely after he died. "And I will receive you, and will be a Father unto you, and ye shall be my sons and daughters, saith the Lord Almighty" (2 Corinthians. 6:17b-18).

Question: Whose prayer did Abby imitate when she cried for pardon?
Scripture reading: Genesis 45:21-25.

6. As Grandfather Does

Jacob and Anna lived with their little boy, John, in the German village of Berheim. John was blessed with a God-fearing grandfather who had prayed for him ever since he was born. When he was baptized, Grandfather had chosen the name "John" for him saying, "May he be loved by God in time and throughout all eternity."

Grandfather often came to visit little John. Many times he would lay his hand on John's head and say, "The Lord bless you, and keep you as the apple of His eye." Those prayers were not left unanswered.

On Grandfather's sixtieth birthday, John went with his parents to see him. John was very happy to spend the whole day with his grandfather. His father had to go to the farm for the day, but promised to return that evening. A terrible thunderstorm arose, however, which made it impossible for him to return. Therefore, John and his mother had to spend the night at Grandfather's house. John was delighted, but his mother felt uneasy in Grandfather's presence.

When evening came, everyone gathered together. Grandfather opened his large Bible and read a chapter. He then offered up an earnest and childlike prayer out of the fullness of his heart. Everyone then went to bed.

The following morning, Anna left to walk back with her child. It was a lovely summer day, and the walk through the woods was very pleasant. John loved flowers and seldom walked past them without stopping. But today he walked behind his mother as seriously and quietly as though there were not a single flower to be seen. Anna did not feel much like talking either. Her mind was uneasy, but she did not know why.

Suddenly, John stood still, looked up in his mother's face, and asked, "Mother, why doesn't Father do as Grandfather does?"

His mother became somewhat confused. "Why don't you go and look for flowers?" she suggested, and walked on.

So they went on silently, but John was not thinking about flowers. Soon they came to the top of a hill where there was a beautiful view of the distant mountains. Anna sat down to rest for a while, and John sat beside her. "Mother," he said for the second time, "why doesn't Father do as Grandfather does?"

Anna felt impatient. "Well," she answered rather sharply, "What does Grandfather do?"

"He takes the large Bible," said John, "and he reads and prays."

His mother blushed. "You should ask your father about it," she answered.

When they reached home, Father was

not there. He had gone to harvest in a field quite far away and would not be back until evening. John's mother knew this and thought she would put her boy to bed early. She hoped that by morning he would have forgotten his question.

But she was mistaken. As she was going to undress him, he said, "Mother, please let me wait until Father comes home."

At eight o'clock, his father returned. John ran up to him directly and asked, "Father, why don't you do as Grandfather does?"

His father looked surprised. The question was unexpected. "What are you doing up John?" he asked, "Go to bed now; it's late."

John was silent, but went sorrowfully to bed. He got up the next morning with still more sadness. He was a different child from what he usually was. He sat silent and sad at the breakfast table, with his hands folded and head down. He had not touched his milk. "What is the matter, John? Why don't you eat?" asked his mother.

John was silent.

After a little while she asked again, "What is it son?" He looked up at his mother very sadly for a moment and bowed his head again. His father and mother had finished, and his mother was clearing the breakfast table. His mother asked a third time, "John, tell me what is bothering you."

Then the boy answered, "I want so much to pray, Mother; but no one will pray with me. I guess I must pray alone."

This was too much for Anna. Tears filled her eyes. She hurried into the next room to tell her husband what the child had said. But he had heard what John had said, for the door was left open. His conscience was touched. "John is right," he said, "and we are wrong." Then they fell on their knees together for the first time in their married life. They prayed a prayer with few words but with many tears. It was the publican's prayer: "God be merciful to us, sinners!" (Luke 18:13)

The happy day had arrived when little John no longer had to pray alone. Father and Mother now began to bend their knees before the Lord to ask for His mercy and forgiveness. They asked for a new heart and for grace for themselves and their child to live entirely for Him.

Do you love to pray as little John did? You must be thankful for, and attentive during, family prayer at home.

Question: In the chapter in Scripture where the publican prays, who else was praying at the same time? Luke 18:9-14. In the following Scriptures, what advice does God have for families: Joel 1:3; Deuteronomy 6:6-7?
Scripture reading: 2 Chronicles 7;14; Jeremiah 29:13; Mark 11:24; James 5:16; 1 John 3:22.

7. Blind Charles

Charles Graham was the son of poor but God-fearing parents. When he was a little boy he was an active and intelligent child. Naturally kind-hearted and affectionate, he was loved by his little friends as well as his parents and relatives.

But before he was nine years old, a sad thing happened to Charles. When he accidentally broke a large glass bottle of sulfuric acid, he lost his sight, and spent the rest of his life in darkness.

How very sad he and his family were when the doctor told them the news! But his parents prayerfully used this affliction as an opportunity to lead their dear son to the Lord. Charles listened intently while his mother spoke to him of his sinful heart, and the necessity of being born again so that he could enter into the kingdom of God. She told him again of the Savior's love and suffering, of His death upon the Cross, of His triumphant resurrection and ascension into heaven, and of His eternal love for poor, lost sinners who come to Him for salvation. The Holy Spirit blessed these instructions to Charles' heart, and he became a disciple of Jesus before he was thirteen years old.

Although his parents rejoiced at Charles' conversion, they were often troubled as they watched their blind son. While the other children were playing games or reading, Charles would talk with friends who came to visit, or find other ways to busy himself. Charles rarely complained, but his parents wished there was a way for Charles to receive an education.

One day, Mr. and Mrs. Graham heard about the Institution for the Blind, and determined to send him there. In this school, Charles learned to read Braille, care for himself, and do many useful tasks. He was delighted to be able to read. He was especially happy to read God's Word. When he returned home his favorite thing to do was to read the Bible. He had a good memory and memorized many texts.

Charles loved to read his Bible, but he was eager to do something for others. He decided to visit some of his sick neighbors and people who couldn't read, in order to read the Bible to them. When Charles told his parents, however, they worried. "How can you do that by yourself?" fretted his mother. "Suppose you were to get lost!"

"Have you prayed about this?" asked Mr. Graham.

"Yes, I've asked the Lord to help me do something useful in His service," answered Charles. "I won't go far, Mrs. Ferris lives two doors down, and she's too old to go out anymore. Maybe she'd like me to visit her and to read to her from my Bible."

"I'll ask James next door if he can go with you, at least until you get to know your way around," decided Mr. Graham.

They all agreed that was a good idea, and so, every day, Charles would visit more and more people in his neighborhood, sharing the Word of God with them. People were especially kind to Charles, for they knew it was not easy for him to go out into the streets. It was a touching sight to see little James holding Charles' hand, guiding him carefully along the sidewalks and helping him find the right doors to knock on. Some of the people Charles visited were children of God; others had never gone to church, or had stopped going to church. Charles would read to them and talk to them about the Savior, and tell them how He saves sinners.

It was not long before Charles became much loved in the community. He cheered many hearts with his kind words and gentle ways, and the Lord blessed his efforts to many souls.

There was one man in the neighborhood named Mr. Jones. No one dared to speak to him about religion. Mr. Jones had been a sailor, and his language was so terrible that people tried to stay away from him as much as they could. His curses and profanity drove people away.

As Charles was passing his door one evening, old Mr. Jones was singing a wicked song. Charles stopped. His heart was filled with pity for this godless man. Charles felt for the door and knocked. When Mr. Jones shouted, "Who is it?" Charles asked politely if he could come in.

Mr. Jones was interested in Charles because he was blind, and asked him many questions. He asked if he could look at his Book and inspected it carefully.

"Can you really read these bumps?" asked Mr. Jones in amazement.

"Yes, sir," answered Charles with a smile. "It took me some time to learn, but I'm so glad I did."

"Read a chapter. I want to see you do it."

Prayerfully, Charles selected a chapter and read it to Mr. Jones. When he finished, Charles spoke earnestly to the old sailor about the danger he was in, and pointed him to Christ as the Savior of sinners. Mr. Jones was touched by the love Charles showed, and asked him to visit him again soon.

Charles was delighted, but spent much time in prayer for Mr. Jones. He visited him every day, and spoke to him about the Lord Jesus, and read from the Bible. Mr. Jones became a "new creature," renewed by the work of the Holy Spirit in his heart. His sins were washed in Christ's blood, and he no longer swore and cursed but spoke of his Savior and the miracle of his conversion. He went to church regularly and served the

Lord faithfully for the rest of his life.

Charles was not strong. The accident which took away his sight had also damaged his health. Slowly he became weaker and sicker, until he had to remain in bed. He always spoke of the love of God and the Lord Jesus Christ, and how he needed the work of the Holy Spirit in his heart. His last hours on earth were triumphant, and the last words he spoke were, "Come, Lord Jesus, come quickly."

Are you a child of God? Do you do anything in God's service? It is not right to "stand all the day idle" (Matthew 20:6). Ask the Lord to use you, for "the night cometh, when no man can work" (John 9:4).

If you are not converted to God, do you realize how much God-fearing parents, teachers, friends, and pastor care about your soul? Surely you ought to care about your own salvation! What will you do, if at last you must say, "The harvest is past, the summer is ended, and [I am] not saved" (Jeremiah. 8:20)? "Is there no balm in Gilead; is there no physician there? why then is not the health of the daughter of my people recovered?" (Jeremiah 8:22).

Questions: How did Charles manage to read the Bible to Mr. Jones? Do you read your Bible as eagerly as Charles did?
Scripture readings: Ecclesiastes 9:10 & Matthew 20:1-16.

8. Bob, the Cabin-boy

A ship sailed from England with a young boy on board. His name was Bob, and it was his duty to serve the captain in any way he could. Bob did not have an easy position, since the captain of this ship was so wicked that even the hardened crew was disgusted with him. It was so bad that some of the sailors were plotting to murder the captain because of his cruel treatment of the men. But they never carried out their plan because the captain suddenly became ill. The first mate took over the charge of the ship, and the sailors carried out their duties, not bothering to care for the sick captain.

Bob, the cabin-boy, could do nothing for the captain. He was now working for the first mate, who kept him very busy. At first, Bob thought the captain just had a passing illness, and that he would soon recover, but after several days Bob learned that the captain was very ill. His young heart was touched to hear that the captain was suffering. He worried about the fact that no one was caring for him so he determined to visit the captain as soon as he got an opportunity.

After supper, Bob softly knocked on the state-room door and carefully opened the door. "Captain?" he whispered. "How are you?"

"What do you care?" snarled the captain. "Get out of here!"

Trembling, Bob closed the door and left. When he knelt by his bed that night, Bob prayed for the captain, and asked God to give him courage to visit the captain again. The next morning, he went again to the captain's room.

"Captain? Are you feeling any better?" Bob asked.

The captain looked surprised to see Bob. "Bob, what are you doing here again? I thought I scared you off. I've had a bad night," he admitted.

"Let me help you," urged Bob. "I can wash your hands and face. It will make you feel better."

The captain nodded silently. Having done his task, Bob suggested, "Let me get you some clean sheets and some clean clothes for you."

Gently, Bob helped the captain into his bed. The kindness of this boy found its way to the captain's heart and tears filled his eyes. "Thank you, Bob," he said quietly.

After that, Bob visited the captain whenever he could. It was clear that the captain was not getting better, but rather worse every day. He began to think of eternity. One day, when Bob entered his room, he said, "Bob, I'm dying. I'm worried about my soul. I'm afraid I will go to hell. I deserve it—I've been such an awful sinner. I'm a lost man."

"But captain," replied Bob. "Jesus Christ can save you!"

"No, Bob, I don't believe that I can be saved. What a sinner I have been! What will become of me?"

Bob did all he could to encourage and comfort the captain, but it was all in vain. "Next time I will bring my Bible," promised Bob.

The following morning, Bob came with his Bible. The captain smiled. "You must read something to me, Bob," he said. "I want to know whether a wicked man such as I am can be saved, and how that happens."

"What shall I read?" asked Bob.

"I don't know. I've never read the Bible myself. Try to find some places that talk about sinners and salvation."

The boy read for two hours, while the captain listened with the eagerness of a man on the verge of eternity. Every word conveyed light to his mind and his astonished soul soon beheld sin as he had never seen it before. The justice of God struck him with amazing force, and although the captain heard Bob read about the Savior, still he could not understand how God could save a sinner like he was. All night long he thought about the passages

Bob had read to him, but they only depressed and terrified him.

The next morning, when the boy entered the state-room, the captain exclaimed, "Oh Bob, I shall never live to reach the land. I am dying very fast. Soon you'll have to throw my body overboard, but that doesn't concern me. It's my soul I'm worried about! I will be lost forever! Can't you pray with me? Please pray for your poor, wicked captain."

The boy hesitated, but then did as the captain asked. Bob dropped to his knees beside the captain's bed, and begged God to have pity on his poor dying master. The captain was deeply touched by Bob's sincere, simple prayer.

The captain added his own prayer. "God, be merciful to me, a sinner," (Luke 18:13) he prayed.

In the evening, Bob read to the captain again. The captain listened eagerly, drinking in every word. The next morning, Bob noticed a change on his master's face. Gone was the despair and sadness, and in its place was a holy calm. "Bob, dear boy," said the captain, "I have had a wonderful night! After you left, I was thinking of all the things I had heard from the Bible. I thought of the Lord Jesus Christ, bleeding on the Cross. I cried out, 'Jesus, thou Son of David, have mercy on me!' And He said to me, 'Son, be of good cheer; thy sins are forgiven thee' (Matthew 9:5). What a miracle! He forgave me my sins! I can believe the promises. His blood has cleansed even me! I am not afraid to die now."

Bob listened with tears in his eyes. "I am happy for you, Captain, but I will miss you when you are gone."

"Do not be sad, Bob," smiled the captain. "I am happy now. You have been so kind to me when I didn't deserve any kindness. God will reward you for it. You have been an instrument in God's hands for my salvation. He sent you to me. God bless you, my dear boy. I am sorry to leave you in such a wicked world and with such wicked sailors. I pray you will be kept from the sins which I have fallen into. Serve the Lord while you are young, Bob, and don't waste your whole life like I have done."

The captain then asked Bob to gather the crew around his bedside. One by one, the captain asked their forgiveness for his cruel ways and sinful behavior. He talked to them about the Lord Jesus Christ, who saves the chief of sinners.

The following morning, Bob went to the captain's room. Quietly he opened the door. It seemed the captain was still sleeping. But when Bob approached the bed, he saw that the captain had died. His soul had left his body, and had gone to be with his blessed Redeemer. Bob was sad to lose his new friend, but he was happy when he thought of the captain now in the presence of his Savior.

Children, it is best to seek and serve the Lord when you are young. You will be kept from much sin and grief if you follow the Lord from your youth. Sin brings no joy, only pain, unhappiness, and bitter consequences. Only those who know and love the Lord Jesus Christ have true joy and peace. The world promises so much: fun, entertainment, pleasure, self-satisfaction, and wealth. But God offers eternal blessings in Jesus Christ that will never fade or deteriorate: peace, joy, love, forgiveness, and eternal life. Do not be foolish and turn your back on God. Turn to Him and ask Him to fill you with His renewing grace. He will never ignore such a prayer.

Question: What happened to the Captain's soul when he died?
Scripture reading: Ecclesiastes 12.

9. Christmas in a Logging Camp

Long ago, a large ship sailed from Scotland on its way to America. The passengers on this ship were people who had heard that life was better in this new land of promise.

Mr. and Mrs. Thompson, with their small son, Robert, were among the passengers on this ship. The young father was eager to start a new life in this new country.

When the ship docked, the Thompsons gathered their meager belongings, and made their way out of the busy city to search for a small farm. After several days, they were able to locate a farm which was for sale. It was just what they wanted, and the purchase was quickly made. Enthusiastically, Mr. Thompson set to work. There were fields to plow, land to clear of trees, animals to care for, and a house and barn to erect.

But the little family's happiness was short-lived. Mr. Thompson became very sick, and soon died. Anna Thompson was now a widow in a strange land, with a small child to care for and a farm to manage. What a frightening situation!

Anna, however, knew what to do. She

told the Lord all her worries and fears. And God heard her and cared for her. Neighbors were friendly, and helped whenever they could. As Robert grew older, he gradually did more and more of the work, and before long he was running the farm his father had only dreamed of.

Anna loved her son and spent many happy moments with him. They worked together cheerfully. In the evenings Anna read aloud God's Word, teaching him about sin and his need for salvation. When he was a child, Robert listened with interest and asked many questions. But as he grew older, he formed a friendship with a neighbor boy whose family did not care about God and His laws.

With great sadness Anna noticed that Robert admired these people and began following their example. No matter how earnestly Anna warned him, Robert would not listen. If his conscience bothered him, he pushed it away, and though he loved and respected his mother, he continued in his own way — away from God. Anna prayed much for Robert till the day she died, but it seemed her prayers would go unanswered.

After his mother's death, Robert became more and more wicked. He drank, he swore; he did not care for any of God's laws. Finally, he ended up in prison. But he told himself he didn't care, and hardened his heart.

In spite of his wicked lifestyle, he was a pleasant young man, and eventually Robert gained the confidence of the jailer. So, when a group of so-called "well-behaved" prisoners was sent to a logging camp, Robert was among them.

While he worked, Robert had time to think. He tried not to think of his sweet, praying mother who had warned him tearfully against his wicked lifestyle. These thoughts condemned him, and he did not like feeling guilty. Memories of the evenings spent studying God's Word with his mother awakened his conscience. Long-hidden texts he had memorized as a child came to mind, but they did not make him happy.

In the city, miles away from the remote logging camp, lived Reverend Craig, whose task it was to visit the logging camps in the forest. Every few weeks, when the weather was good, this faithful minister would set out on horseback to visit the prisoner-lumberjacks. He traveled from camp to camp through the thick forest, carefully winding his way along deep ravines and the pine-needle carpeted trails. Wherever he went he brought the Word of God in a simple yet forthright manner. Reverend Craig was eager to reach the hearts of these rough, lonely men. They too had souls created for eternity, and the pastor spent much time in prayer for these prisoners.

With Christmas approaching, Reverend Craig set out for the logging camps. Dandy, his fine black horse, was hitched to a sleigh in which the pastor was seated; he was wrapped in warm furs. It was a beautiful day. Snowflakes floated soundlessly to the snow-covered forest floor. Small animals darted out of the way as the horse effortlessly pulled the sleigh over the snowy trails. Occasionally, Reverend Craig had to get out of the sleigh to clear the path of fallen branches.

After two days of travel, he reached the logging camp, where he was heartily welcomed. Eagerly the prisoners and guards accepted the small packages Mrs. Craig had so thoughtfully sent for each of them. Some of the men spoke with the pastor about the Savior they had come to know and love. The Lord had blessed Reverend Craig's work with the prisoners, and it cheered his heart to hear some of the men show by their words and lives that they now belonged to God.

In the evening, after a simple supper of stew and bread, the loggers assembled together in the crude log cabin which served as the cafeteria and meeting hall. Robert Thompson was among the men gathered to hear Reverend Craig's message.

The pastor read the well-known story of Jesus' birth, and explained to the men why it was necessary for God to send His beloved Son to be born in Bethlehem, and why He had to die on Calvary. He talked about how unworthy we are of this miraculous gift. Afterward, without having planned to do so, Reverend Craig shared the story of his own conversion.

"When I was young," began Reverend Craig, "my mother taught me Bible stories, and taught me about the Lord. But after my mother died, I forgot all about God and His commandments. I lived in sin until the Lord stopped me. I felt my sins were like a mountain. There was no peace for me, for I could not get rid of my mountain of sin.

"One Sunday I casually walked into a church. The minister there preached from Matthew 1:21: 'And she shall bring forth a son, and thou shalt call his name JESUS: for he shall save his people from their sins.' I saw that there was a way to be saved in Jesus, God's gift to His people. Jesus Christ, born the King of kings, saved me from my sins. And He can save you too! You are not too sinful, or too old, or too young to be saved. He saves sinners!"

Reverend Craig bowed his head and said, "Let's pray." The men folded their hands and bowed their heads. Several fell to their knees in true repentance. But Robert sat quietly, unable to move. Reverend Craig's story sounded like his—the first part, that is. He had rejected his mother's teachings, and now he too felt as though his sins were like a mountain, standing between God and himself. He felt as though he were drowning in a river of guilt. Needless to say, Robert slept poorly that night. The next morning Reverend Craig made preparations to leave the logging camp. He had just stepped into the sleigh when Robert approached.

"Robert," called the minister kindly, "what can I do for you?"

Looking anxiously at the pastor, Robert asked, "Is it true what you told us last night?"

Immediate understanding caused the pastor to breathe a quick prayer for guidance. "You mean, when I said no one is too sinful to be saved?"

Robert nodded. Reverend Craig could see the hunger for hope in the eyes of this desperate prisoner.

"Listen, Robert. Jesus Himself said that He did not come to call the righteous, but sinners to repentance."

Robert hesitated. "But is that for someone like me, too?"

"Mr. Thompson," replied Reverend Craig, "I know only that it is for sinners who humble themselves before God and are sorry for their sins. Are you a sinner?"

An anguished look came over the haggard face of this miserable man. "But you don't know who I really am! You don't know what I've done!" he moaned.

"Don't tell me!" cried Reverend Craig. "Tell the Lord, who knows everything already! Do not be afraid, Robert, to pour out your heart before Him," he added gently.

Robert remained silent, and Reverend Craig urged his horse forward. The horse hadn't taken ten steps before he heard Robert calling after him, "If it is not true what you're telling me, then I am damned to hell forever!"

Reverend Craig stopped Dandy and called back to Robert, "If that which I've told you is not true, then everyone is damned to hell forever. If Christ does not save sinners, then all men are lost forever, even those who have believed in Jesus Christ."

The minister picked up the reins and Dandy started out again. At the bend in the road, Reverend Craig looked back and saw a beautiful sight: Robert Thompson kneeling in the snow with his arms stretched toward heaven. The forest soon hid Robert from the happy pastor's sight. Reverend Craig did not need to hear about the result of that prayer, for he was well acquainted with the God who gives and answers penitent prayers. He trusted that Robert would be able to tell him next time he saw him, "Blessed be God, which hath not turned away my prayer, nor his mercy from me" (Psalm 66:20). And he believed that the angels in heaven were singing because of this one sinner on the forest path, who was pouring out his heart before God.

Question: Why didn't Reverend Craig need to wait to hear the result of Robert's prayer?
Scripture reading: John 3:1-21.

10. Family Worship

One morning before leaving for work, Mr. Watson told his family that Mr. Cole would be staying with them for the night. Mr. Cole was coming to visit Mr. Watson to discuss some business matters.

"Does he have any children?" asked Michael.

"Yes, he has one little daughter," replied Mr. Watson, "but she is staying at home with Mrs. Cole."

"Is he a Christian?" Anna wanted to know.

"I'm afraid not," said Mr. Watson. "He is a kind man but not a Christian."

"That's too bad," commented Mrs. Watson. "People who do not love the Lord are not happy people."

After work, Mr. Watson brought Mr. Cole with him. They enjoyed a delicious meal together. When they were finished, Michael carried the big family Bible to his father.

"Mr. Cole," said Mr. Watson, "we are in the habit of having family worship after supper. You are welcome to join us, or you may wait for us in the living room."

"I'd like to stay, if you don't mind," replied Mr. Cole with a smile.

Mr. Watson read a chapter from the Bible, and the family sang and prayed together.

Because business took longer than expected, Mr. Cole stayed with the Watsons for several days before heading back to his family.

The Watsons did not hear from Mr. Cole for several years. Then one evening, there was a knock on the door. Mrs. Watson opened it and exclaimed, "Mr. Cole! How nice to see you again! Please come in!"

The family greeted him warmly, and the friends exchanged news. But after a little while, Mr. Cole said, "I did go out of my way a bit because I really wanted to visit you again. I have some news that will make you very happy. I am now, by God's amazing grace, a Christian."

After the Watson's expressions of joy, he continued. "It all started with my visit here. When I heard the Bible read, and prayed along with you, it was the first time in years that I had heard God's Word, or prayed. I had a godly mother when I was a boy. She died when I was only nine years old. My father was not a Christian, and soon married a woman who was not a Christian either. I thought I had forgotten all my mother's teachings, but when you read from the Bible and prayed to the almighty God in heaven, it all came back. I loved my mother very much, and those times I spent with her were happy times. When I came home, I bought a Bible and began reading it. I started going to church with my family. I asked God to renew me, and to help me be the kind of husband and father you are, Mr. Watson. At first it seemed God was not answering my prayers. I became sad and distressed! My sins bothered me so much that I could not sleep some nights. But then the Holy Spirit applied a text my mother had taught me: 'The blood of Jesus Christ His Son cleanseth us from all sin' (1 John 1:7b). I have found the Lord to be faithful to His promises, and now I am truly happy."

"I will greatly rejoice in the LORD, my soul shall be joyful in my God; for He hath clothed me with the garments of salvation, He hath covered me with the robe of righteousness, as a bridegroom decketh himself with ornaments, and as a bride adorneth herself with her jewels" (Isaiah 61:10).

Question: How was Mr. Cole's conscience awakened? It is good to spend time thinking about God and learning about Him. Worshipping God as a family is a wonderful thing to do. Malachi 3:16-18 tells us that God remembers those who think upon His name. What does God describe His people as in verse 17?
Scripture reading: Joshua 24:14-28.

11. Given to the Poor, Lent to the Lord

One morning in a New England village, a poor man asked his pastor for money. The minister asked his wife if they had anything to give the man.

"This is all we have," said the wife to her husband, "forty-eight cents."

"Have faith in God," answered the minister. "He could give us forty-eight dollars in place of those forty-eight cents!" The minister was a cheerful giver. So let's see what came of it.

About an hour later, a wealthy friend of the minister who lived some distance away, called to see him with his servant. They had come to town on business. He stopped at the minister's house to get something to eat while they visited. But this gentleman noticed, while he was eating lunch with them, how sad and downcast the minister's wife seemed. He asked what was wrong, but the lady avoided giving an answer, and soon left the room. Then the gentleman asked his friend, the minister, if they were in need of money, but the minister only smiled and said nothing.

As soon as the gentleman was alone with his servant, he asked him if he had any money with him, and how much. They both looked into their wallets to see what they had with them. The gentleman discovered he had forty-five dollars, and his servant had only three. He wished very much that he could find two dollars more in his pockets, so that he could give the minister the round sum of fifty dollars. But this was all they had with them.

Then the gentleman took the forty-eight dollars, and gave them to the minister, saying, "I am sure, my friend, that you are short of money. I would like to have given you fifty dollars, but this is all we have."

The minister was overcome with surprise and joy. He counted out the money on the table, and called in his wife. "Look and see how soon God has acted! He did not even wait till the day was past, but through our kind friend here has sent us forty-eight dollars for the forty-eight cents we gave to that poor man this morning!"

Then they told their friend all about it, and he was delighted to find that he had neither more nor less than what was just sufficient to repay the good minister a hundredfold for what he had so cheerfully given to the poor man that morning. They thanked and praised God with humble, joyful hearts.

Question: How many times greater was the repayment that God sent the minister?
Scripture reading: Mark 10:28-30.

12. Hindering God's Work

A business man in a large city said to one of his friends one day, "I wonder why none of my employees have become Christians. I've talked to them about going to church and believing in God. But none of them are interested it seems."

"If you will allow me to be honest," began the man's friend, "I think I know the answer."

The business man looked up in surprise. "Go ahead, tell me!"

With a sigh, his friend began, "You know that you have a very bad temper. You often speak harshly to your employees, and find fault with them, when often they are not to blame. This makes them doubt whether you are sincere in your Christianity. You, my friend, are the reason they are not interested."

The businessman made no answer. Deep down in his heart, he knew his friend had spoken the truth. "Thanks for being honest with me," he said in a sad voice.

The man went home. He went to his room and knelt by his bed. Convicted by the Holy Spirit, he confessed his sins to God and prayed for forgiveness. Then he asked

God to help him overcome his bad temper, and to be gentle and kind as Jesus was.

The next morning, the business man called all his employees into his office. With tears, he apologized to them for his bad temper, and asked their forgiveness. He told them that he wanted to walk in the ways of the Lord Jesus. Then he prayed with his employees.

After that, his employees never saw any more bad temper on the part of the business man, and before long, several of them began attending church. They began to respect their boss, and to take his religion seriously. They saw that God forgives sin and helps His people fight against it. "Wherefore he is able also to save them to the uttermost that come unto God by him, seeing he ever liveth to make intercession for them" (Hebrews 7:25).

Question: How can you stop your behavior that hinders God's work?
Scripture reading: Ephesians 6:5-9.

13. How Kindness Helped a Boy

Miss Mason had just started a job as a school teacher in a little country school. Her mother had died when she was a little girl, and her father had just passed away a few weeks before she began teaching. This was her first teaching job, and she felt nervous and a bit scared. She had heard about the behavior of some of the older boys. She prayed for help, and asked the Lord to give her strength and patience.

Joe Stanton was considered the worst boy in the community. He was an orphan, and lived with a family who seemed to value him only for the work he did for them. He was rude and involved in all kinds of mischief.

The first day of school did not go very well. Joe was loud and uncooperative. He ignored Miss Mason when she asked him to do an assignment, and was disrespectful. Poor Miss Mason! She did not know what to do. He was much taller than she was, and she did not know how to make him obey her. She bowed her head and asked the Lord for His almighty help.

When school was dismissed, she asked

Joe to help her clean up. Surprisingly, he stayed to help. It did not take long to straighten out the room, and they were soon ready to head home. As they walked along together, Miss Mason tried to think of something to talk about.

"Do you have any brothers or sisters, Joe?" she asked kindly.

Unknowingly, Miss Mason had touched the only tender spot in Joe's heart. "I had a sister," he answered softly. "Mary was my only sister. I used to take care of her and play with her. I took her for rides in a wagon I made for her. She loved me more than anyone else ever did. She used to run to meet me when I came home." He paused, then added quietly, "But she's dead now, and nobody cares about me anymore. Her grave is over the next hill in the cemetery."

"Would you like to show me her grave, Joe?" asked Miss Mason gently.

Joe looked up in surprise. "Do you really want me to?"

"Yes, Joe, I do. My mother died when I was a little girl, and my father died just a few weeks ago."

They walked on slowly, talking about little Mary. They reached the grave, and sat down on the grass nearby. Joe had been wiping away the tears as they trickled down his cheeks, one by one. But now he sobbed out his grief. "She's dead, Miss Mason, and nobody cares about me anymore!"

"I care, Joe," said the teacher, putting her

hand on his shoulder.

Then she spoke to him about the Lord Jesus, who is the Friend of the fatherless, and of His love for children. She spoke of her own loneliness, and how the Lord was her dearest companion. She confessed that teaching school was difficult, and that she would need the Lord's help.

Joe looked at her. "Miss Mason, I'll help you. I'll do whatever I can to help you. I'm sorry for being rude today."

"Thank you, Joe," answered Miss Mason.

And so it was. Joe helped Miss Mason, and when the other children saw that Joe was so kind and helpful and obedient, they followed his example. The children grew to love their teacher, and learned lessons not only from their books, but from the Bible and from the piety seen in their dear teacher.

Question: Which description of Jesus did Miss Mason use to comfort Joe?
Scripture reading: Psalm 68:1-10.

14. I Cannot Get Away From God

Many years ago, a young man named John lived in London. He was a servant for a wealthy family. He earned enough money to live comfortably and he had a kind master, but there was one thing which troubled and annoyed him. It was that his mother lived nearby and that she visited him often. Perhaps you wonder why this should bother him so much. The reason was, that whenever she came, she spoke to her son about the Lord and the salvation of his soul. John always felt very uncomfortable when his mother talked to him about death and being prepared to die. He did not like to hear that he needed to be born again. He thought life would be dreadfully boring if he were to become a Christian.

"Mother," said John at last, "I cannot stand this any longer. Unless you drop that subject altogether, I shall quit my job and move away, so I won't have to listen to this kind of talk anymore!"

John's mother was sad to hear this. But she did not give up. "My son," she said, looking up into his face, "as long as I have a tongue, I shall never stop talking to you about the Lord, and to the Lord about you."

John did just as he said he would. He

wrote to a friend in the Highlands of Scotland, and asked him to find him a job there. John knew that his mother could not write (and in those days there were no telephones), so he felt as though he had escaped. John was sorry to leave his good job in London, but he told himself he needed peace and quiet.

John's friend found a job for him in a gentleman's stables. John did not care that his mother saw how glad he was to get away from her. It made his mother sad, but she knew she could still pray for him.

John's new employer was also a kind man, for which John was thankful. He enjoyed working with the fine horses in the spacious stables. John felt that at last he had gained the peace and quiet he desired.

The day after he began his new job, John noticed his master observing him as he worked with one of the horses. "I think he wants to see if I know what I'm doing," thought John to himself. "Well, he'll soon see what a good worker I am."

Suddenly, the master asked, "John, are you saved?"

John turned pale with shock. He felt simply terrified. "God has followed me to Scotland!" he thought. "I could get away from my mother, but I cannot get away from God!" And at that moment he knew how Adam must have felt when he tried to hide himself from the presence of God behind the trees in the garden.

John could not answer his caring master; he had to stop working, he trembled so badly. The master noticed the fear in the young man and led him to a bench. He sat beside him in silence for a few moments; he then began to speak. So once again, John heard the old, old story so often told him by his mother. But this time it sounded new, for it had become real to him. How angry God must be with him for running away! How great was his rebellion! And the Savior who came to suffer and die for sinners—how great was John's sin in despising and rejecting such a Savior! How he had grieved the Holy Spirit who had been knocking at the door of his heart for so many years! For the first time, John felt that he was a lost sinner before a holy God.

By the time the master had stopped speaking, John felt sick, due to the conviction of sin and fear that had come over him. His agony was so great that he had to stop working for the rest of the day.

But the faithful master did not leave John to himself. He understood what John was experiencing and was eager to share with John the way of salvation. He continued to speak with John and to pray with and for him. Soon the love and grace of the Savior became as real to John as the grief and sorrow over his sins. John learned there was mercy also for him. He saw that the blood of Jesus cleanses from all sin.

The first letter John wrote to his mother

was to tell her the joyful news, "God has followed me to Scotland, and He has saved my soul!" Can you imagine the joy of the godly mother?

"Whither shall I go from thy spirit? or whither shall I flee from thy presence? If I ascend up into heaven, thou art there... If I take the wings of the morning, there shall thy hand lead me, and thy right hand shall hold me. If I say, Surely the darkness shall cover me; even the night shall be light about me. Yea, the darkness hideth not from thee; but the night shineth as the day: the darkness and the light are both alike to thee" (Psalm 139).

Question: Who did John say had followed him to Scotland? How did God stop Jonah from running away from Him? In Ruth 1:15-18 do you read about someone who is the same as or opposite to Jonah?
Scripture reading: Jonah 1 & 2.

15. John's Sacrifice

Steamboats used to travel on Lake Erie carrying passengers from one side of the lake to the other. A steamboat had a large boiler below deck that burned wood or coal to make steam to run the boat. "The Swallow" was a large steamboat that could hold many people.

One beautiful day, "The Swallow" was about halfway on its run that usually took one-and-a-half hours. Some of the passengers were seated, and others were strolling along the deck. They were enjoying the beautiful trip. No one was thinking of any possible danger. But suddenly a large cloud of smoke billowed up from beneath the boat.

Captain Jones was the first to see the smoke. "Sam!" he called to one of the crew, "quickly go below deck and see what is causing all that smoke!"

Sam did as he was told but returned at once, pale and filled with terror. "Captain! Captain!" he shouted, "the boat is on fire!"

Several of the passengers also heard Sam and began to shout, "Fire! Fire!"

Captain Jones quickly took command. "Everyone on deck!" he ordered. "Seamen!

Pour on water!" His orders were followed immediately. Streams of water were poured onto the fire. But the boat was loaded with tar, which burns easily and makes a very hot fire. It was, therefore, impossible to put out the fire with water.

The passengers began to panic. "Captain, how far is it to land?"

"About a mile and a half," he answered.

"How long will that take?"

"At the rate we are going, about forty-five minutes."

"Will we make it? Are we in danger?"

"We are in great danger. Everyone, go to the back of the boat! Most of the fire is at the front."

Everyone hurried to the back of the steamboat except old John Maynard who remained at the wheel, steering the boat towards land. Captain Jones called through the smoke, "John! John, can you hear me? What direction are we going?"

"South-southeast!" came the reply.

"Steer Southeast to the nearest coast!" returned the captain.

Black clouds of smoke continued to pour from below deck. Flames began to lick their way around the front of the boat. After some time, the captain called again, "John! John! Are you still there?"

"Here, Captain," was the reply. But his voice was growing weaker.

"Can you hold out for five more minutes? We are almost to land."

"I will try, Captain, with the help of the Lord."

The hair of the old man was already singed, and parts of his body were badly burned. His right arm was charred, but his left hand was steady on the wheel. He stood as firm as a rock in the middle of the smoke and flames. He had to steer the boat to land to save his captain and all the men, women, and children on board the boat.

At last the boat reached land. The captain, passengers, and crew scrambled from the burning vessel. John, too, was helped ashore. But as everyone gathered around him, he sank down on the shore and died. What a sad sight this was! Grief filled the hearts of the people. There lay the one who had saved them. John had given his life so that they could live. Thankful tears filled their eyes.

The captain and all the crew members and passengers attended the old man's funeral. A large crowd from the city also came. As the coffin was lowered into the grave, many tears fell.

A beautiful marble headstone was placed on John's grave. Engraved on the stone in gold letters are the words:

John Maynard
The Man at the Wheel
From the Thankful Passengers of
"The Swallow"
He Died For Us!

John Maynard was certainly a hero. He did not spare himself, but saved those on board the steamboat. In this way he is similar to the Lord Jesus. But Jesus did much more for His people. Jesus freely gave Himself, knowing that He would die the most painful and shameful death on the cross. This was necessary to save His people from an eternal death. But the grave of the Lord Jesus is empty, for He has risen again. He has ascended into heaven to pray for His people there. If you may know, by the grace of God, that He died to save you, then you too will be truly blessed—both now and forever.

Question: Why did Jesus go to die on the Cross?
Scripture reading: John 15:12-17.

16. No Treasure in Heaven

Two Christian friends visited a wealthy farmer in Illinois one day to ask him to donate money for mission work. The farmer was friendly and showed them around his farm. Then he took them up to the cupola (a small tower) on the top of his house. From this point the men could see for miles. The farmer pointed out all the fields that belonged to him, the barns, the herds of horses, the sheep, and the cattle.

"Those are all mine. I started out as a poor boy, helping on someone's farm, and now I own all this property."

One of the Christian men pointed to heaven and asked, "And how much treasure have you laid up in heaven, my friend?"

After a pause, the farmer admitted with a sigh, "I'm afraid I haven't got anything there."

"Isn't that a dreadful mistake?" asked the Christian man. "You are a man of ability and intelligence and yet you have spent all your time gaining treasure on earth while neglecting to gain treasure in heaven."

The farmer was silent for a moment, then said, with tears in his eyes, "I have been foolish, haven't I?"

"Lay not up for yourselves treasures upon earth, where moth and rust doth corrupt, and where thieves break through and steal: but lay up for yourselves treasures in heaven, where neither moth nor rust doth corrupt, and where thieves do not break through nor steal: for where your treasure is there will your heart be also" (Matthew 6:19-21).

Question: Why was the intelligent farmer so foolish? What are we told to love or have affection for in Colossians 3:2?
Scripture reading: Matthew 19:16-26.

17. Not Now – But Later!

One day a Christian doctor called to see an old man whom he had frequently visited. The doctor had spoken many times to old John and his wife about their souls. John listened attentively and said he agreed with the truth explained to him, but always seemed to want to avoid the deeper personal truth of the matter. He would admit that he was a sinner and that he needed to be saved. He would even say that he intended to seek the Savior some day. He wished to be saved, but was putting it off for a "more convenient season."

Now John was suffering from bronchitis. He was in no serious danger, but felt painfully weak and ill. The doctor examined him and promised to prepare some medicine which they could have someone pick up. He was about to say "goodbye" when John's wife asked, "When must John take the medicine, Doctor?"

"I will put the directions on the label," replied the doctor. Then, turning to his patient, he said, "Let me see; you are not very ill; suppose you begin to take the medicine a month from today?"

John coughed to show how much he needed the medicine and almost choked. "A month from today!" he sputtered.

"Yes, why not? Is that too soon?"

"Too soon! Why, sir, I may be dead then," groaned old John.

"Quite true," agreed the doctor, "but you must remember that you are not very bad yet. Still, perhaps you had better begin in a week's time."

"But, Doctor!" cried John greatly puzzled and troubled, "I might not live a week!"

"That is very true," the doctor agreed, "but probably you will, and the medicine will be in the house. It will keep, and if you find yourself getting worse, you could take some then." He eyed the old man calmly as though there was nothing at all strange in the directions he was giving.

John groaned; never had his doctor dealt with him in such a strange manner! As if giving in somewhat, the doctor added, "If you should feel worse tomorrow, you might even begin then."

"Sir," the old man said desperately, "I may be dead tomorrow! Oh, Doctor," he went on more quietly, for indeed his throat and chest were painful, "I hope you won't be angry with me, nor think me ungrateful. You've always been good to me, but you know, sir, I don't want to get worse. I believe the medicine is good, but it will do me no good while it is in the bottle. It is foolish and senseless to put off taking it, isn't it?"

"When would you suggest to begin then, John?"

"Well, sir, I thought you'd tell me to begin today."

"Begin today, by all means," said the doctor, and for the first time he smiled. "I only wanted to show you how foolish your own reasoning is when you delay asking for the more valuable medicine which the great Physician has provided for your sin-sick soul. Just think how long you have neglected His remedy! For years you have turned away from it. You have said to yourself, 'Next week or next year, or when I am about to die, I will seek the Lord – any time rather than the present.' And yet today is the only time you are sure of. God's medicine is for 'today.' 'Now is the accepted time; behold, now is the day of salvation.' The remedy is near, but it will do you no good unless it is given to you. It is so foolish to put off asking for this even until tomorrow."

Old John's eyes were full of tears as he pressed the hand of his kind friend. "I never saw it this way before," he whispered.

Question: It is foolish to ignore God's earnest call to repentance. Why is it so dangerous to delay and plan to seek God at a later time? Why did the doctor suggest that John delay taking his medicine?
Scripture reading: Acts 24:22-27.

18. Poor John the Stone-breaker

A wealthy Englishman was riding through his estate. Suddenly he stopped his horse. He thought he heard someone speaking. Looking over the hedge, he saw a poor man. For many years this poor man had been hired to break stones for the rich man's roads. Therefore this man was called 'John the Stonebreaker.'

The rich man called to his poor workman, "I say, John, what are you talking to yourself about?"

"Please, sir," said John, "I wasn't speaking to myself. I was just asking God's blessing on my dinner."

The rich man laughed. "And what have you got for your dinner, John?"

"Well, sir," replied John, "I've only got a crust of bread and a mug of pure water from the brook, but sir," he continued, "it's a good meal when God blesses it."

"Well, well," answered his master as he prepared to ride off, "it would be a long time before I'd ask God's blessing on a dinner like that. I wish you much good from your blessing, John. Good day." Away he rode on his tour of inspection.

Still, John enjoyed his dinner in spite of

what his wealthy employer had said. The rich man did not know of the wealth which was hidden in John's heart. As a true child of God, John had a lasting treasure laid up in heaven.

Not long after this happened, the rich man was taking a short walk in a green field near his mansion. He suddenly stopped and turned pale. He stood trembling with fear. "What's that I hear?" he exclaimed. "'The richest man in the county shall die tonight!'"

He listened and again thought he heard the same words repeated: 'The richest man in the county shall die tonight!'

Greatly alarmed, he began to think of who was the richest man in the county, and finally came to the conclusion that he was the richest.

Hurrying home, he asked for his doctor to come immediately. He seriously begged the doctor to do all he could to save his life. The doctor was very surprised. He did not see anything wrong with his patient! The rich man, however, kept thinking that he was going to die that night.

But why all this excitement? It was the power of the rich man's accusing conscience showing him how unprepared he was to die.

Restlessly, he tossed upon his bed all night. There was no sleep for him. At last the grey dawn appeared. The doctor, who had not left the rich man's side, finally persuaded him to get up and take a walk before breakfast. When he did go out, he was pale and trembling. He expected that at any step he might drop dead.

He had not gone far, however, when he was met by a poor workman who touched his cap respectfully and said, "Please, sir, may I speak with you?"

"Of course you may," was the reply.

"Well, sir," answered the workman. "I thought I should tell you that poor John the Stonebreaker was found dead in his bed this morning."

"What's that?" asked the rich man in great surprise, "John the Stonebreaker died?" After thinking about this, he exclaimed, "Ah! I see it now! I see it now! I thought that I, with my many acres, my mansions, and my gold, was the richest man in the county, but poor John the Stonebreaker, with his crust of bread and mug of water and God's blessing, was by far the richer man."

Whether or not he took this serious lesson to heart, we do not know. May God grant, however, that you and I shall do so!

Question: Who was the "richest man in the county" and why?
Scripture reading: Luke 16:19-31.

19. Repaying Good for Evil

Once there was a godly man named Stephen Savery. He owned a general store in town. One night someone stole some of the things from Mr. Savery's store. Although he thought he knew who had stolen the items, Mr. Savery decided to publish an ad in the town's newspaper. This is what it said: "Whoever stole some flour, coffee, sugar, canned goods, and some farming tools from the General Store on the fifth day of August, is hereby informed that the owner has a sincere wish to be his friend. If poverty tempted him to commit this sin, the owner will keep the whole transaction secret and will gladly help him find a job so that he no longer needs to steal."

When the thief, named Miles Lynden, read this advertisement, he was surprised. His conscience spoke against him, and he began to feel ashamed of himself.

A few nights later, the Saverys heard a knock on their door. There stood Miles Lynden with a bundle over his shoulder. Without looking up, Miles said, "I have brought these back, Mr. Savery. Where shall I put them?"

"Come on in, Miles," said Mr. Savery. "Tell me how this happened. Then we can figure out how we can help you."

Mrs. Savery prepared some hot coffee and other refreshments. "Here is something to fill your stomach," she smiled.

Miles turned his back towards them and did not speak for a few moments. After a while he said in a quiet voice, "It is the first time I ever stole anything, and I have felt very bad about it. I never thought I would come so far as to steal something. Ever since I started drinking, things have gotten worse and worse. You are the first people who have offered me a helping hand. My wife is sick, and my family is hungry. They need new clothes. I know you've helped whenever you could, and yet I stole from you. I'm sorry."

"I hope you never steal again," responded Mr. Savery. "This secret will remain between us. You are still young, and with God's help, you can make up for lost time. Promise me, Miles, that you will not drink any wine or liquor for a year, and I will hire you to work in my store starting tomorrow. Your oldest son can come and work with us after school. Eat a bit now. Perhaps it will keep you from craving anything stronger when you get home. You will find it hard to stay away from the liquor at first, but be strong for the sake of your wife and children, and it will soon become easier. When you need some strong coffee, tell Mary and she will always give you some. Remember the Bible verse, 'Wherefore take unto you the whole armour of God, that ye may be able to withstand in the evil day, and having done all, to stand' (Ephesians. 6:13). Think often of this passage too, 'Submit yourselves therefore to God. Resist the devil, and he will flee from you' (James 4:7). Spend much time in prayer and in the Word of God."

Miles was overwhelmed at the kindness of these people. How was it that they were willing to help someone who had wronged them? "Why are you doing this?" he asked, his eyes filling with tears. "I never did anything good for you!"

Stephen and Mary Savery smiled. "It's what the Savior did for us, Miles," explained Mrs. Savery. "We did nothing good to Him, but in His great mercy He saved us."

"We are to be like Jesus," continued her husband. "Keep close to God. Work hard and stay away from the liquor, Miles, and you will always find friends in us."

The next day Miles Lynden came to work, and by God's grace, he became an honest, sober, faithful, God-fearing man. He continued working for Stephen Savery for many years. Miles never forgot the kindness the Saverys showed him that night, and he thanked God every day for forgiving his sins and making him a new creation.

Question: Why did the Saverys help Miles?
Scripture reading: Hebrews 13:1-6.

20. Susan's Prayer of Faith

Susan was a widow who had a small daughter named Mary. Susan was a true Christian and longed for little Mary to be converted too. She tried to teach her child about the Lord and the way of salvation. She read to Mary from the Bible and helped her memorize many verses.

But Mary did not enjoy the Bible lessons. She would squirm and fidget impatiently until the lesson was finished. Then she would rush out to play with her friends as soon as she was free.

One Sunday, Mary ran off with some neighbor's children. She had not asked for permission, and her mother was very worried. When Mary finally came home, Susan sat down with her to explain how seriously wrong her behavior was. "Mary," she said, "you must remember that today is Sunday. Today is the Lord's Day. You must not run and play with your friends, but stay with me. I will read to you from the Bible. And we will pray to the Lord and ask Him to give you a new heart."

But Mary would not listen and was very rude to her mother. Susan was very sad to see Mary so disobedient and stubborn. Susan went to her room feeling very troubled and distressed. Kneeling by her bed, she began to sob as she prayed to the Lord for her dear daughter. She begged the Lord to give Mary a new heart.

Alone in the kitchen, Mary heard her mother's voice. She first thought her mother was telling someone else how bad she had been.

Mary quietly crept up to her mother's door and peeked through the keyhole. To her surprise, her mother was alone. She saw that her mother was praying for her! But her mother's prayer did not cause Mary any concern. She was only relieved that no one was with her mother. Mary quietly crept away again and ran off to play with her friends, quickly forgetting her mother's words.

Several years passed and Mary became a young lady. She was even more stubborn and willful than when she was younger. She married and had a family, but she was not kind to her husband and was a poor mother for her children. Her God-fearing mother passed away soon after Mary's wedding. Until the end of her life, she had prayed in faith that Mary would be converted.

Mary moved to the country far away from any church. She put her mother's Bible away. She never read God's Word to her children. Then Mr. Walters, a Christian, moved into the neighborhood. He saw the need for starting a Sunday School for the many children in that area. But he did not know of a place where they could meet.

He decided to call a meeting to ask the parents whether they would like to have a Sunday School. Many parents were very thankful to have a Sunday School started for their children. They gladly agreed to take turns using their homes for a meeting place. Mary did not want her home to be used and she did not want her children to attend, but she was afraid of what her neighbors would think of her, so she agreed to take her turn.

Mary did not go to Sunday School with her children as most of the other parents did. And when the Sunday School met at her house, she tried to disturb the class as much as possible. She would walk around the room slamming cupboard doors, banging pans, and being as noisy as she could. Mr. Walters tried to speak to Mary about this, but Mary wouldn't listen. She just kept trying to disturb the classes as before. Mr. Walters did not want to upset her even more, so he decided not speak to her about it anymore.

A few months later, however, everyone was surprised to see Mary quietly standing in the doorway, listening to Mr. Walter's lesson. The next Sunday, Mary came with her children to Sunday School and again stood listening quietly. Finally, after several weeks, Mary came, bringing her mother's

Bible with her. She sat down with the children and took her turn reading a verse from the Bible.

Mr. Walters thought it best not to speak to Mary at first, but soon he heard from others how much she had changed. He then approached her and said, "Mary, you seem so different. Has something happened in your life?"

"Oh, yes!" she replied. "I *am* different. And it's all because of Jane."

"Jane?" asked Mr. Walters in surprise, looking at Jane, Mary's six-year-old daughter. "But she is just a child!"

"Yes, Jane! It was something that she did. One day I saw her peeking through a keyhole!

"When I was a child like Jane, I behaved very badly. I would not listen to my mother and did many wicked things on Sunday. One Sunday after my mother scolded me, I heard her talking to someone. I thought she was telling someone about how bad I was, so I crept to her door to listen. Then I peeked through her keyhole and saw that my dear mother was praying for me! She was begging the Lord to give me a new heart. I laughed at her then and have always lived as I pleased. But when I saw Jane looking through the keyhole, it reminded me of how sinful I am! It reminded me of my mother's prayers for me. How could God have spared me from judgment for so many years? Seeing my daughter peeking through that keyhole made me realize that she has never seen her mother pray. My great guilt brought me on my knees in prayer for the first time in my life. I prayed and prayed that God would be merciful to me, a sinner."

Mary's eyes filled with tears as she continued earnestly, "And God heard me. He did not cast me off, even though I have been so wicked. He has graciously answered my mother's prayers and has given me a new heart."

The change in Mary was real and could be seen by everyone. The Lord forgave Mary for the sake of the Lord Jesus Christ who died for her on the Cross. He clothed her in His righteousness.

Susan did not live to see the answer to her prayers. But the Lord knew what was best for Susan, and He knows what is best for each of His children. When Susan died, the Lord took her to be with Him forever where she found eternal fullness of joy.

Question: Why did seeing Jane look through the keyhole affect Mary so dramatically?
Scripture reading: James 5:13-18.

21. That's You, Jim!

Mr. Carr owned a book shop. It was not like most other book shops because Mr. Carr was a Christian and sold mostly Christian books. In the large window that faced the street he placed an attractive display of Bibles.

One day a group of men passed by. They had painted their faces and wore wildly colorful costumes. They earned money by entertaining people on the streets. They stopped right in front of Mr. Carr's book shop and began their show. They sang some silly songs and acted out a funny story. When they had finished, one of the young men held out a hat and asked the audience for some money. With a prayer in his heart, Mr. Carr took one of the Bibles from his window display and approached the young man.

"I will give you ten dollars, and you may keep the book too, if you read aloud a portion of it so everyone can hear," he said.

The young man laughed. "What an easy way to make ten dollars! Listen, folks! I'll read to you!"

Mr. Carr opened the Bible at the fifteenth chapter of Luke, and pointed to the eleventh verse. "Start right here."

"Now, Jim, speak loudly," called one of his friends, "and earn your ten dollars like a man!"

The people laughed. Jim took the book and began to read in a theatrical voice.

"And he said, A certain man had two sons: and the younger of them said to his father, Father, give me the portion of goods that falleth to me. And he divided unto them his living."

Something had changed in Jim's voice. He was no longer reading in a comical way. The audience noticed the change in Jim and listened more closely.

"And not many days after, the younger son gathered all together, and took his journey into a far country, and there wasted

his substance with riotous living."

"That's you, Jim!" exclaimed one of the friends. "It's just like what you told me about yourself and your father!"

Jim did not respond, but continued reading.

"And when he had spent all, there arose a mighty famine in that land; and he began to be in want."

"Why, that's you again, Jim!" said the same man. "Read on!"

"And he went and joined himself to a citizen of that country; and he sent him into his fields to feed swine. And he would fain have filled his belly with the husks that the swine did eat: and no man gave unto him."

"That's like all of us, Jim!" said his friend, interrupting once again. "We're all beggars and are having a hard time. Read on! Let's hear what happens."

The young man read on, and as he read, his voice trembled.

"And when he came to himself, he said, How many hired servants of my father's have bread enough to spare, and I perish with hunger! I will arise and go to my father, and will say unto him, Father, I have sinned against heaven, and before thee, and am no more worthy to be called thy son: make me as one of thy hired servants."

At this point, Jim broke down and could read no further. All the people in the audience were impressed; some shed tears. Mr. Carr moved to stand beside Jim, and took the Bible from the weeping man. He continued to read where Jim had left off.

"And he arose, and came to his father. But when he was yet a great way off, his father saw him, and had compassion, and ran, and fell on his neck, and kissed him. And the son said unto him, Father, I have sinned against heaven, and in thy sight, and am no more worthy to be called thy son. But the father said to his servants, Bring forth the best robe, and put it on him; and put a ring on his hand, and shoes on his feet: and bring hither the fatted calf, and kill it; and let us eat, and be merry: for this my son was dead, and is alive again; he was lost, and is found. And they began to be merry."

Hearing this clear story of the gospel, Jim was filled with hope. His father and mother loved him, and perhaps they would welcome him back.

Suddenly a new thought struck Jim. Not only was he living in poverty; he was living in sin. Like a flood, his sins came to his memory, and all hope left him. He was poor physically and spiritually!

That day was the turning point in the life of this prodigal son. Mr. Carr became his dear friend, and the Bible a constant companion. Mr. Carr encouraged Jim to write to his parents. This resulted in the joyful reunion of Jim and his parents. But even better was the reconciliation Jim experienced with his heavenly Father. He found that God was as ready to receive him as the father in the parable was to receive his son, and Jim was greatly humbled by it.

"O the depth of the riches both of the wisdom and knowledge of God! how unsearchable are his judgments, and his ways past finding out!" (Romans 11:33)

Question: Which parable did Jim find so striking and why?
Scripture reading: Isaiah 1:16-20.

22. The Power of a Short Sermon

Dan was a soldier in the British army. He was rude and disobedient, rough and unkind. He cursed and swore. He was not afraid to sin. The commander tried to change Dan's behavior, but he could not. Finally Dan had to go to prison and solitary confinement. That means he was put in a small room on his own. No one was allowed to visit him or even speak to him. Only a minister could visit him.

This was very hard for Dan. Now he had no one to whom he could swear or tell jokes. Two weeks passed by. Dan spent those weeks bitterly swearing against God. The chaplain, or army minister, tried to talk with Dan several times. Everything he said was met with anger and curses. Finally the chaplain gave up. He went to an old minister and told him about Dan. The old minister said he would try to talk to Dan.

The old minister went to see Dan in the morning. When he stepped inside Dan's cell, Dan shouted, "If you're going to preach to me, I don't want to hear it!"

The minister answered kindly, "I'd like to pray with you, Dan." Without waiting for Dan's answer, the minister began to pray.

But Dan yelled and cursed so loudly that he didn't hear a word. The minister stood up to leave. Never had he met a man so full of hatred and anger. A silent prayer rose in his heart for Dan. He signalled to the guard that he was ready to go. As the guard opened the door, the minister turned to look at Dan and said to him quietly but sternly, "Young man, the wages of sin is death." (Romans 6:23)

Then the door clanged shut. The minister left, but his words did not. The Holy Spirit applied these words with power to Dan's soul. Over and over the words ran through his mind: "The wages of sin is death; the wages of sin is death."

Finally Dan couldn't take it any more and cried out, "God, be merciful to me, a sinner!"

How surprised the old minister was to hear that Dan had asked him to come again! With great joy he taught Dan the last part of the verse, "but the gift of God is eternal life, through Jesus Christ our Lord." What a miracle this was for Dan! Salvation was possible, even for such a great sinner as he!

Dan's conversion was real and lasting. He lived to be a good soldier of Jesus Christ. He loved to speak about the grace of God for unworthy sinners, for he knew that God is able to save the chief of sinners.

Question: Why did the minister's words affect Dan so dramatically?
Scripture reading: Isaiah 49:8-13.

23. "To Ruin"

One summer evening a man was trying to find his way home through the streets that led to his house. He was so drunk that it was impossible for him to find his way home.

Quite unable to tell where he was going, he at last swore loudly and said to a man going by: "I've lost my way. Where am I going?"

The man answered in a compassionate voice, "To ruin."

The next day, when the effect of the drink had passed away, those two words, tenderly and lovingly spoken to him, did not pass away. "To ruin! To ruin!" the poor man kept whispering to himself. "It's true! I'm going to ruin! Oh God, help me and save me!"

In this way, he was stopped on his way of sin. He earnestly sought God in prayer for the grace which changed his life.

Question: Why was "to ruin" a short but true answer to this man's question?
Scripture reference: Matthew 7:13-14.

24. A Boy and a Principal

There was once a boy named Bradley who was in the seventh grade. He had been sent to the principal's office so many times that at last he was told to report to the office after school. The principal told Bradley to write down all the things he had done wrong in school that year. Bradley was busy for quite a while. When he was finished, the principal read the list. Next, Bradley had to write a sentence or two explaining why he had done these things.

By this time, Bradley was beginning to get a good idea of his bad record at school. At last he was finished. He was tired and hungry, and wanted to go home. But the principal had one more request.

"Now," he said, "take a fresh sheet of paper and copy it out so we can send it to your mother."

When he heard this, Bradley began to cry. "Please, sir, don't send it home to my mother," he pleaded.

"Why not?" asked the principal, "doesn't your mother already know all these things?"

"No, she doesn't," answered Bradley.

"Does she think you are behaving well at school?" questioned the principal.

"Well, she knows that I get into trouble sometimes, but not this much," Bradley said, pointing to the paper in front of him.

"So, you don't want your mother to know about your behavior at school," said the principal thoughtfully, "but I don't see how we can help it. We tried to get you to change your behavior. Let me think a minute."

The principal got up and walked around the room for a few moments as Bradley wiped away his tears. Then he sat down in his chair. "Bradley, could you be the sort of boy your mother would like you to be?"

Bradley looked up, surprised. "Yes, I think I could, sir," he answered slowly.

"Well, I'll tell you what we will do. We will put the paper you have written in an envelope and seal it. We'll lock it in my drawer here in the office. If you are not sent to see me again for the rest of the school year, we will destroy the envelope with the paper in it, and say no more about it."

Bradley was dumbfounded. "Thank you, sir," he stammered.

Bradley did his best to behave after that. He asked the Lord to help him. It was very difficult at times to restrain himself, but God helped him.

This is something like what God does for His people. It is as though He writes down all our wicked thoughts, words, and actions. But because of the Lord Jesus Christ's sacrifice for sin on the Cross, the Lord forgives His people all their sins, and

He does not remember them anymore. In Psalm 103, David says, "He hath not dealt with us after our sins; nor rewarded us according to our iniquities. For as the heaven is high above the earth, so great is his mercy toward them that fear him. As far as the east is from the west, so far hath he removed our transgressions from us" (Psalm 103:10-12).

Are your sins washed away? Do you long to have your sins forgiven? There are many beautiful promises given by God to encourage us to ask Him for forgiveness. That is why He sent His only begotten Son, to pay for the sins of those who come to Him for mercy. "Who is a God like unto thee, that pardoneth iniquity, and passeth by the transgression of the remnant of his heritage? He retaineth not his anger for ever, because he delighteth in mercy. He will turn again, he will have compassion upon us; he will subdue our iniquities; and thou wilt cast all their sins into the depths of the sea" (Micah 7: 18-19). "Come now, and let us reason together, saith the LORD: though your sins be as scarlet, they shall be as white as snow; though they be red like crimson, they shall be as wool" (Isaiah 1:18).

Question: What does God do with our sins when we by grace trust in Jesus Christ alone for salvation? Acts 3:19
Scripture reading: Isaiah 44:21-28.

25. A Little Child Shall Lead Them

S

A minister of the gospel, who lived in England, had a careless, idle son. He left his parents, being tired of their religion and earnest warnings, got a job on a ship, and sailed on a long voyage over the Atlantic Ocean. His distressed parents grieved over him, and followed him with their prayers and with godly advice in their letters to him.

The ship on which this young man sailed anchored, during the course of the voyage, in the harbor of one of the beautiful islands of the Atlantic. They stayed there for some days, taking in cargo. One day, the sailors took with them on the ship a little native boy, who could play an instrument the sailors had never seen before. The sailors were fascinated, and the boy was happy to play for them.

At last, the boy asked the sailors to please bring him to shore again. But the sailors wanted him to stay longer.

"Oh," cried the little boy, "I really must go! A good Christian missionary has come to the village where I live. From him I have learned all I know about Jesus Christ, in whom I wish to believe. He always meets us at this time of the day, in the shade of the big tree, to tell us more about Jesus. And I want to go and hear him!"

The sailors were quite touched with the earnestness of the boy, and at once rowed him ashore. But that thoughtless son of the English minister was especially struck by the words of this native boy. He could not stop thinking about those words. They penetrated deeper than his conscience, right into his heart.

"Here am I," he said to himself, "the son of a minister in England, knowing far more about Jesus Christ than this poor boy, and yet not caring about Him! This little fellow is now earnestly listening to the Word of Life, while I am neglecting it!"

He went to his bed that night in great distress of mind. He wept bitter tears over his sins and prayed to be forgiven. His prayer was heard and answered. He became a child of God, and great was the joy of his parents when the news reached them. Their son, who had been dead, was alive again, and he who had been lost was found!

Question: Do you act on the privilege of Bible teaching that you have been given?
Scripture reading: Matthew 21:12-17.

26. Becky's Prayer

B ecky tugged at her mother's skirt. "Mommy, am I born to die?"
Becky's mother was surprised to hear such a serious question from her small daughter. She was busy feeding the baby, and gave Becky a quick response. "Yes, Becky, we all have to die."

"But can't I do something so I won't die? What if I'm very, very rich, or very, very good? I don't want to die," she said firmly, shaking her head and searching her mother's face.

At that moment baby Sarah started to cry, requiring the mother's attention. She took the baby on her lap while she spoke to Becky. "No, dear, you can't ever get away from death. Everyone who is born must die sooner or later. But God can take away the fear of death and change your heart so that you will be wiling to die. He can save you from your sins. The Lord Jesus said, 'Suffer little children to some unto Me, and forbid them not, for of such is the kingdom of God.'"

Sarah was finished with her feeding, and the conversation ended there. Becky was barely four years old and did not understand much of what her mother had just explained to her, but the words, "God can take away the fear of death" stuck in her mind. Now she wondered, "Will God do that for me? How do I ask Him? Will He listen to me?"

Becky remembered hearing a poem that her mother had read to her several times:

> *God is in heaven*
> *And will He hear*
> *A little child like me?*

That was Becky's question. But she couldn't believe the last part of the poem:

> *Yes thoughtful child*
> *Thou needst not fear*
> *He listeneth to thee.*

She had heard her father read the Bible often. She had been impressed with the story of the giving of the law on Mount Sinai. God was so holy and just and majestic. She was sure that God was angry with her for her sins.

One day Aunt Martha came to visit Becky's mother. While Becky's mother was getting tea ready, the little girl went over to her aunt and sat on her lap.

"Aunt Martha," she began, "how do you pray?" Becky's solemn blue eyes met her aunt's.

The question rather annoyed Aunt Martha. She felt that her sister was far too religious. Although she herself attended church, she did not approve of "overdoing it." She felt that too much religion just made a person feel miserable.

"How do you talk to God?" Becky persisted, patting her aunt's hand.

The woman really did not know what to say, for she had never breathed a true prayer in her life. Suddenly she remembered that her Prayer Book was still in her purse. She pulled it out and handed it to Becky. "There are lots of prayers in this book, dear. I think this will help you."

"But I can't read!" exclaimed Becky, tears forming in her eyes.

"Well," sighed Aunt Martha, "come to my house tomorrow and I'll help you memorise one or two of them."

Becky was glad for the promised help, and her aunt was relieved that she asked no more questions. Becky's mother came in with the tea and the conversation drifted to other topics.

The next day Becky went to visit her aunt and worked hard at memorising two of the prayers from the little Prayer Book. Aunt Martha was impressed at the diligence and sincerity with which Becky attempted to commit them to her memory. Secretly she thought it would be healthier for Becky to be playing outside with her friends.

That night before Becky climbed into bed, she tried to recite the prayers she had learned. But, try as she would, she could not remember every part of them, and the parts she did recall made no sense to her at all. They made her feel more miserable than ever. She wanted to know God, but she didn't know how that could ever be.

The next day she decided she would ask her mother. She went into the kitchen where her mother was baking cookies. Before Becky could begin speaking, her mother said, "Becky could you please bring this basket to Mrs Noble? She has a bad headache again, and I really don't have time to go there myself." So Becky went.

After supper she planned to ask her father how she could get to know the Lord, but he left for a meeting before she had finished clearing the table.

On Sunday the whole family went to church. Becky couldn't understand the sermon, although she did her best to listen. Near the end of the sermon, the minister said something that Becky did understand: "If you find you cannot pray, ask Him to teach you how." Becky thought about this all the way home. Then she went quietly to her bedroom and kneeled by her bed. "Gracious God in heaven," she whispered, "please teach me how to pray so that I can know thee. Amen."

Much later, Becky was able to say that the Lord had heard that prayer and taught her how to pray. Where there is a cry for mercy, the merciful Lord will hear and answer.

Question: Who did Becky find to help her pray?
Scripture readings: Luke 11:5-13.

27. How God Used a Drought and an Umbrella

S

There was a severe drought some years ago in the northern part of England. The situation became so severe that if it would not rain within a week, the crops would be totally lost. Due to this urgent need, it was decided to have a special prayer service for rain in one of the local churches.

As the minister of this congregation was approaching the church, he saw a little girl ahead of him carrying an umbrella. He caught up with the girl and asked her, "My little girl, why are you carrying an umbrella to church on such a hot day?"

Turning and looking into his face, the girl answered, "We are going to ask God to send rain today. I want to be ready."

The minister testified in his sermon that the faith of this girl put him to shame.

Question: What kind of faith did Jesus say that we need to enter the kingdom of heaven?
Scripture reading: Luke 18:15-17.

28. "Man, Do You Love God?"

An old, ragged tramp knocked at the back door of a New Hampshire home one morning and asked for something to eat. The mother invited the poor old man into the kitchen to rest, and while preparing a good meal for him, she learned that at one time he had had a good home and a wife and children.

Drink had driven him from one sin to another until his family deserted him. He then drifted from place to place and deeper and deeper into sin until he had nothing left to do but beg. He believed that no one cared what became of him and that it didn't matter much to himself either.

The small son of the woman sat near the table watching the old man. Finally he walked over to the man and placed his little hand on the man's dirty, ragged coat sleeve and looked up into his face. "Man, do you love God?" he asked. He repeated the question several times but received no reply.

The little boy then went to his room and returned with a little money that had been given to him for candy. He placed it in the hand of the old man saying, "Man, this will buy you some bread." The poor man bowed his head and cried, touched by the little boy's generosity.

He left the house and was not heard from for many months. At last a letter came addressed to the child saying, "Little one, you saved me from hell. After I left your house, I walked along the road, and all I could hear was, 'Man, do you love God?' I fell asleep that night under a tree and dreamed of a fair, curly-haired boy, with his hand on my sleeve, saying over and over, "Man, do you love God?"

"That was all I could hear and see for days, until I threw myself on the ground and cried all the hardness out of my heart. I saw again the man I used to be, the cozy home I had owned, the loving wife and the dear children that sin had taken from my side. I thought of all I had sacrificed to serve the devil and of what I had become. I cried out to God to save my soul and to wash away my sin.

"I have a job now and clothes, and a place to sleep. I'm an old man. I won't be here long, but God bless you, child, because by grace you led an old dirty tramp back to God."

Question: How can you touch someone near you with kindness?
Scripture reading: 1 Samuel 17:1-58.

29. Robert Learns a Valuable Lesson

Little Robert Manly was only about five years old. Yet, young as he was, he liked to have his own way. He thought a great deal about pleasing himself, which is not at all the best way to be happy.

A very poor family lived down the road behind the Manlys' house. The father of this family was a drunkard. He was very cruel to his wife and children, and often beat them.

One day this poor woman came to Robert's mother to beg for a little fresh milk for her baby girl. Mrs. Manly had none to spare except what she had saved for Robert's supper. But when Mrs. Manly took one look at the baby and saw that she was actually slowly starving to death, she happily gave away the milk.

At supper time Mrs. Manly told Robert about the starving baby and how she had given his milk away. Robert was not pleased. He pouted and cried and refused to eat any of his supper. He said the milk was his and nobody should have it.

With a heavy heart, Mrs. Manly sent Robert to bed. She spoke to him about what Jesus wants us to do, and that selfishness is sin. That evening she lifted up her heart in prayer to God that He would take away these bad feelings in her son's heart, and give him a heart to love and serve God.

The next day she took Robert with her to visit this poor family, thinking that the sight of their misery would do him good. So they went down the road together to visit the drunkard's family. How cold and shabby everything seemed there! It made Robert shiver to look around in that cheerless home. It made him feel very sad.

The poor woman thanked Mrs. Manly and Robert over and over again for the fresh milk. "It kept the baby quiet all night," she said. "Her father didn't beat her, for he beats her when he comes home drunk and finds her crying. Oh, my poor child!" The woman began to weep, and said, "She can't help it! She's just hungry!"

Mrs. Manly put her arm around the woman's shoulder. "I don't know if I can spare any more milk. I want to very much but–"

"Oh, no!" cried the woman, "you musn't give me any more of your child's milk. He needs it!"

"Is there anything else I could do for you?" asked Mrs. Manly kindly.

"Nothing, thank you," replied the woman. "The most you could do is to find some more fresh milk," she sighed, kissing her baby.

As they walked home, Robert didn't say

a word, though he was usually very talkative. He seemed to be thinking earnestly about something. His mother said nothing, but prayed in her heart that God would teach him to feel and do what was right.

At supper time Robert's glass of milk was set by his plate. He did not immediately come to the table, but sat staring into the fire as if he hadn't heard.

"Come, Robert," said his father.

He obeyed, but gently shoved his milk to one side. In a few minutes he went to his mother and said in a whisper, "Mommy, may I take my milk to the baby?"

"Yes, my son," she answered, giving him a hug.

Once again, mother and son took a short walk down the road to their neighbor's home. They soon returned. Robert ran to his father and shouted happily, "The baby's got the milk, Daddy! Now she'll sleep! Her mother said to me, 'God bless you, child!' And, Mommy, my milk tastes very good tonight — I mean my 'no milk!'"

Robert had learned that "it is more blessed to give than to receive." It made him happier to give his milk to the poor baby than to drink it himself.

Question: Did Robert lose out by giving away his milk?
Scripture reading: Acts 20:32-38.

30. The Shepherd Boy and the Lost Sheep

One evening at the close of a cold February day in a small Irish village, there was a knock on the door of a little house. The farmer who lived there opened the door.

"Come in out of the cold, sir," he said. "What can we do for you?"

"Well, sir, ma'am," said the man, addressing the farmer and his wife, "if it's not too much trouble, could I spend the night? I am a minister and I live a few hours' journey from here. I was visiting some people and stayed longer than I planned. There is a storm brewing and I thought I'd better find a place to stay."

"Of course you're welcome to stay!" exclaimed the farmer's wife. "Come right in and we'll take care of you."

She immediately warmed some stew for the minister. She sat with him at the kitchen table while he ate. The farmer and his wife also had a son, about twelve years old, who listened quietly while the others talked.

It wasn't long before the pastor discovered that these people had never read the Bible and had never had the gospel explained to them.

Just then the boy began to cough.

"You have a bad cough," commented the minister.

"Yes sir," replied the boy.

"How did you catch that cold?" asked the pastor kindly.

"A week ago, one of our sheep went astray, and my father sent me to search for it. The snow lay thick upon the ground. The cold seemed to go right through me, but I didn't mind it much because I really wanted to find that sheep."

"Did you find it?" asked the pastor with interest.

"Oh yes! I never stopped till I did!"

"And how did you get it home?" asked the minister.

"I just laid it on my shoulders and carried it home."

"And were your parents happy to see you?"

The boy smiled. "They certainly were! Father, mother, and even the neighbors were glad."

"Wonderful!" thought the minister to himself. "Here is the whole gospel story. The sheep is lost. The father sends his son to seek it. The son goes, seeks, suffers, finds, lays the lost sheep on his shoulders, brings it home, and rejoices over it with friends and family."

The minister opened his Bible and read aloud Luke 15:4-7. At once they saw the resemblance to the boy's experience. They then listened with great interest as the pastor explained the meaning of the parable.

It was the Lord's set time to work. The Lord graciously opened their hearts to receive the gospel. They understood, repented, and believed in the Lord Jesus Christ who is the Good Shepherd who laid down His life for His sheep. And there was rejoicing over these lost sheep which had been found and brought back to the heavenly fold of the Great Shepherd.

The King of love my Shepherd is,
Whose goodness faileth never;
I nothing lack if I am His
And He is mine forever.

Perverse and foolish, oft I strayed,
But yet in love He sought me,
And on His shoulder gently laid,
And home, rejoicing, brought me.

Question: Which of Jesus' titles does this story remind us of?
Scripture reading: Luke 15:1-7.

31. The Little Kitchen Maid

Long ago most people had servants. Rich people had many servants, and the less rich had fewer servants. The butler was the most important servant. He decided what meals to serve, answered the door, and was in charge of the other servants. The lowest servant was the kitchen maid. She had to make sure the fires were going when it was cold or time to cook, and she scrubbed the floors and washed the dishes. Often the kitchen maid was an orphan, and very poor.

In a beautiful home in Scotland a little kitchen maid carried in a bundle of sticks. Carefully, she put the sticks into the oven, one at a time. "It's about time you tended that fire, Katy. It's almost out."

Katy was used to the cook's harsh remarks, and said nothing. Instead, she brushed away the ashes which had fallen out of the oven and then wiped her hands on her threadbare brown dress. It was the only dress she owned. She hoped to buy a new one as soon as she had saved enough money. This was her first week at her first job, and she might be able to afford it after two months. Katy hoped that her master, the pastor of the village, would be pleased with her work. She decided she would do her very best.

Katy was just taking off her apron after her work when she heard footsteps approaching the kitchen. The door opened and the butler entered. "Katy," he said, "Reverend McDowell wants to see you."

Katy's face must have turned white, for the butler took her by the hand and said kindly, "Come with me, little one. He's not at all angry with you."

Katy wanted to ask why he wanted to see her, but she didn't dare. The butler led her up the back stairway into the parlour, where the McDowell family was sitting. Katy wished she was at home with Gramma.

"Come, Katy," said the pastor. "I'd like you to join us for a little while."

Katy looked bewildered. This was unheard of! Kitchen maids were never asked to enter the parlour, or sit with the family they worked for.

"Come, sit beside me," urged the minister.

"Don't you think she needs a bath first?" suggested Mrs. McDowell. Katy could tell that she was uncomfortable having a dirty little kitchen maid in her parlour. The children whispered and giggled together.

"I'm surprised at you," said the pastor. "'The Lord looketh on the heart.' We are all in need of the same thing."

A tear slid down Katy's cheek. She would rather not be here. "I could just stand, sir;

then I won't get anything dirty," she said shyly.

Mrs McDowell was immediately sorry she had made such an unkind remark, and made no protest as her husband placed Katy beside him on the couch.

"Katy," Reverend McDowell said, "we are going to read from the Bible. Have you ever seen the Bible?"

She shook her head. In fact, Katy had never heard of the Bible before.

"We'll read something easy enough for you to understand," promised the minister. He chose the story of Adam and Eve, pausing at times to question Katy or explain something she did not understand.

Then he asked each of his four children several questions. At last, Reverend McDowell turned to Katy. "Perhaps this has been a bit hard for you to understand. Let me just ask you a few questions, Katy. Do you know that you have a soul?"

Katy shook her head, then blushed with embarrassment when she saw the astonished looks of the others.

"When God made you, he gave you a soul. When you die, that soul will go either to heaven or hell. Have you heard of those places before, Katy?"

Again Katy shook her head, and even the minister was surprised, but he did not show it. Instead, he said, "Tomorrow evening, come to my study and I will teach you."

Reverend McDowell then prayed for each of his children, his wife, and for Katy. Soon Katy was on her way home, her mind full of questions. Why did she need a new heart? Where was she going when she died? Why didn't Eve listen to God? Who was God, really? She listened with great interest the next evening when the minister answered all her questions. Before Katy went home, Reverend McDowell said, "Katy, I want you to pray this little prayer: 'Lord Jesus, show me myself.' Pray it over and over. Remember, God hears you wherever you are. If you come next week then I will read to you from the Bible."

"I'd like that, sir," replied Katy eagerly.

Before the week was over, however, a little boy knocked on the front door of the parsonage. The butler asked him what he wanted. The boy stammered, "I— I — I'm Katy's brother, and— and she's sick, sir!"

"Oh," said the butler. "Wait a minute, and I'll call Reverend McDowell."

Soon the pastor came to the door. "What is your name, son?" he asked smiling.

"Neil," he answered. "I'm Katy's brother. She can't work today. She wanted to but Gramma said she was too sick."

"Did the doctor come to see her, Neil?" inquired Reverend McDowell.

Neil shook his head and whispered, "We don't have any money for a doctor. But Gramma's good at taking care of her."

"Where do you live, Neil?"

144

The minister wrote down the address and called the butler. "Call Dr. Blair and tell him I'd like him to see Katy at this address. Don't worry, Neil," said Reverend McDowell, "the doctor won't ask you to pay. But take me with you, and we'll go and visit Katy."

As they walked, Reverend McDowell spoke to Neil about the Bible and Neil's need of a new heart. He was pleased to discover that Katy had told her brother what she had learned at the pastor's home. Soon they came to the place where Katy and Neil lived with their grandmother. The streets were dirty and the houses run down. They climbed the creaky stairway that brought then to the attic room of the two orphans.

Neil was bursting with pride as he announced, "I brung the preacher!"

An old woman shuffled from the single bedroom and said quietly, "Good morning, Reverend. It's very kind of you to come here. Katy has been talking about you for days. She'll be glad to see you."

The minister approached Katy's bed. It seemed as though she was asleep.

"Katy," said Rev McDowell softly.

She opened her eyes. "Oh!" she said in surprise. "How did you find us?"

"Neil brought me," he stated. "How are you feeling?"

A shadow passed over Katy's pale face. "Not very good, sir. I've been praying the prayer you taught me, and it didn't make me feel happy at all."

"How did it make you feel, Katy?" asked Reverend McDowell kindly.

"Like Eve. I'm not a good girl. Before, I thought I was good because I did my best for Gramma and for you. But I'm such a sinner, and I think God is very angry with me. I don't dare pray that prayer anymore. I'm afraid God will put me right into hell!"

"Katy, listen. I will teach you another prayer: 'Lord Jesus, show me Thyself.' Say it to God over and over again until you get peace. Remember, God hears prayer, Katy."

Reverend McDowell left her then and returned home, all the while pleading with God to answer Katy's prayer and give her His peace. A few days later, the minister received a letter from Katy's grandmother.

Dear Reverend McDowell,

I'm sorry to tell you that Katy won't be working for you any longer. The kind doctor that you sent here has found a place for us to live. It is at his friend's house. The doctor told us there will be other children for Neil and Katy to play with. They will even have a yard to play in. They will have to do a few chores to earn their keep, and I will do what I can to earn a bit of money. Thank you for your kindness to us.

Mrs. Campbell

Slowly Reverend McDowell folded the letter. He thanked God for His goodness to Katy, and prayed for her conversion.

The years passed, and the pastor became an old man. One bright day in September, there was a knock at the door. The butler answered the door and saw a well-dressed lady standing there.

"Could I see Reverend McDowell?" she asked.

"May I ask who is asking to see him?" inquired the butler.

The woman smiled. "Just tell him Katy is here."

The butler turned to go and then stopped. "Katy? The kitchen maid?" Then he laughed. "Well, you sure have changed!"

Soon the old pastor came out and warmly shook her hand. "Tell me all about yourself, Katy. But first, tell me this: did you pray the second prayer I taught you?"

Tears sprang to Katy's eyes. "Yes, sir, I did, and I can never thank God enough for allowing me to meet you. The Lord Jesus showed Himself to me and gave me peace. There have been times when I lost that peace and I would pray that prayer again."

Reverend McDowell spent the afternoon talking about God's wonderful ways in their lives. "As for God, His way is perfect" (Psalm 18:30a).

Question: Dear boys and girls, Will you also pray, "Lord Jesus, show me myself, and show me Thyself?"
Scripture reading: John 16:15-21.

Prayer Points

Faithful Witnesses

1. ★ Thank God for being willing and able to save you from your sins.
    ❖ Ask God to forgive you for the sins of your heart, mind, and body.

2. ★ Thank God for the promise of salvation to His people.
    ❖ Ask God to take your sins away and make you one of His people.

3. ★ Pray to the Lord for friends and family who do not know or follow Him and who are not thinking about the reality of eternity.
    ❖ Ask God to teach you to "number your days" and realize that this life will end one day. Submit your life to Him and ask Him to direct your priorities.

4. ★ Pray that you will be a good influence on others. Pray that your life will be one that shows people how God wants them to live.
    ❖ Ask God to make you open to listening to those who love and follow Him. Ask Him to forgive you for hating instruction and ignoring God's Word.

5. ★ Thank God for hearing and answering your prayers. Thank Him that He knows everything even before we ask Him. Thank Him that His love and care for us means He longs to give us the privilege of speaking directly to Him.
    ❖ Ask God to pardon your sin and forgive you for all your sins, including the sin of unbelief.

6. ★ Pray to God that He will give you a real desire to pray to Him and learn about Him. Ask Him to teach you how to pray to Him as you should.

   ❖ Ask God that He will teach you that real prayer is not just words but a real conversation and search after a mighty God and loving Savior.

7. ★ Thank God for making you a new creation. Pray that the evidence of this change will be seen by others in your life.

   ❖ Ask God to change you from being a lost sinner to a saved sinner. Acknowledge that the only way this is possible is through Christ and His death on Calvary.

8. ★ Ask God to give you directions on how He wants you to serve Him. Pray for those serving Him already as pastors and preachers. Pray for those who support them such as their wives, family, elders, and Sunday School teachers.

   ❖ Ask forgiveness for wasting time instead of giving your time to God. Ask God to make you His and for you to give your whole life to Him.

9. ★ Thank God that you are not too sinful for salvation and that God has called you to repentance. Repent of your sins to Him.

   ❖ Ask the Lord to show you that you are a sinner needing to be saved.

10. ★ Thank God that through Christ you are no longer a filthy sinner in His eyes but clothed in Christ's righteousness.

    ❖ Ask the Lord Jesus Christ to show you your true spiritual condition without Him and make you humble to receive Him and His salvation.

11. ★ Thank God for the gift of His Son, the Lord Jesus Christ. Praise Him for the immeasurable value of this gift that we can never repay. Thank Him for giving this gift to undeserving sinners. ❖ Ask God to give you a clean heart and a faith in Him for life and eternity. Ask Him to show you how you cannot clean your heart yourself by your works.

12. ★ Ask Christ to make you more like Himself with a merciful and loving nature which will not put others off becoming Christians. ❖ Ask God to help you focus on Christ His Son. Ask Him to make you realize that He is the one we need to come to for eternal life. Ask God to take away your excuses.

13. ★ Pray for friends and families who have lost loved ones. Ask God to show you how to help them and show God's love to them. ❖ Ask the Lord to become your dearest companion and best friend. Ask Him to change your heart so that you love Him most of all.

14. ★ Thank God that there is nothing hidden from Him. Repent of your sins and thank Him for His faithfulness and justice. ❖ Ask God to forgive you for your rejection of Him in the past. Ask Him to make you bow your heart and submit to Him in all things.

15. ★ Thank Jesus for the greatest gift He has given and ever could give — Himself. ❖ Ask God to show you that Jesus Christ died for sinners but that His grave is now empty. Ask Him to help you in the big and little problems you may face today.

16. ★ Thank God for the lasting treasures available to His people. Ask Him to help you obtain these and focus on Christ and the Word of God. ❖ Ask God to show you how worthless possessions are and how valuable eternal life is. Ask Him to forgive you and bring you to a realization of what Christ has done for sinners.

17. ★ Thank God for His perfect plan. Thank Him that salvation is offered freely and that Jesus Christ is the one and only rescue plan for sinners and that He is always ready to save the lost. Thank God that He has told you exactly where to go for refuge. ❖ Ask God to bring you to a knowledge of the danger of eternity without Christ and the blessing of eternity with Him.

18. ★ Rejoice in God's love and tell Him how you are grateful for His many physical and spiritual gifts. Thank God for the real and eternal richess available through Jesus Christ. ❖ Ask God to convict you of your selfishness and greed for things that don't last. Ask forgiveness for not treasuring Him and His Word as you should.

19. ★ Thank God for the Savior's great mercy to awful sinners, including yourself. ❖ Ask God to help you resist the devil and temptation today and for the rest of your life.

20. ★ Thank God for His perfect timing and that He always answers prayers when they need to be answered and in exactly the right way. ❖ Ask God to forgive you and your stubborn nature. Ask Him to make you surrender your whole life to Him.

21.　★ Thank God for His love to sinners that is as a father loves His child. Thank Him for loving disobedient children like us, and for being willing to forgive.

❖ Ask God to help you start on a journey of discovery of God's wisdom and the depth of His riches. Ask Him to make you realize your own foolishness and spiritual poverty.

22.　★ Thank God for eternal life and that you don't earn it but just submit yourself to Christ. Pray for missionaries in situations where the gospel is fought against. Pray for their safety and the advancement of the good news of Christ.

❖ Ask God to forgive you. Ask Him to take away the love of sin which destroys your life.

23.　★ Thank God for deliverance from sin and for the gift of life that He gives so abundantly. Thank Him for joy and peace. Pray for countries who are at war or where terrorism destroys life. Pray that the Word and truth of Christ will guide these countries in the future.

❖ Ask God to show you in your life and the life of others the danger and destruction of sin. Ask Him to show you in your own nation where God must be honored.

24.　★ Thank God for His love and patience and for His delight in mercy. Seek His love and compassion today. Ask God to help you show His love to neigbors and friends and to make your community a place where Christ is King.

❖ Ask God to forgive your sins and to teach you how you can know for sure that in His great mercy and love your sins are cast away but you are not.

Childhood Faith

25.   ★ Thank God for the opportunity He has given
you to learn about Him. Thank Him for His Word
and those who teach it. Thank Him for books
which explain the Bible and for the freedom to
worship God. Pray for those who try to reach
out to adults and children who have no
knowledge of Christ or God's Word. Pray for
your own family and the future of your nation
and that God will be honored in both.
❖ Repent of the times you have read and
learned about Jesus Christ and yet have not
cared about Him at all. Ask God to make these
instances things of the past and that from now
on you will love and honor Him.

26.   ★ Thank God that He looks on your heart and
nothing else. Thank Him that He loves all who
belong to Him, male, female, all nationalities,
sizes, ages, and backgrounds.
❖ Ask God to help you to pray to Him. Pray
for forgiveness and pray that you will be
known as someone who spends time with
God in a real and meaningful way.

27.   ★ Ask God to give you faith in Him for all your
needs today and in the future. Trust Him for
salvation, your greatest need.
❖ Ask God to forgive you for doubting Him
and not believing in His power.

28.   ★ Ask God to help you ask people the right
questions about their spiritual state.
❖ Ask God to convict you of your own neglect
of your soul and God's Word. Ask God to bring
you to Himself.

29 ★ Ask God to give you a tender heart to other people's needs. Ask Him to help you to give to others in order to honor Him.
❖ Ask God to receive you as a needy sinner as you seek to know and love Him. Ask Him to give you forgiveness for your sins.

30. ★ Thank God that He was the one who sought you and brought you safely to Himself for the salvation of your soul. Thank Him for His patience in bringing you to submit to Him.
❖ Ask God to show you that you will lack nothing if you come to Him and that when you belong to Christ He will be yours forever.

31. ★ Thank God for His perfect ways and for the mercy and grace He has shown you.
❖ Ask God to show you how sinful and needy you are and how holy, just, powerful, and loving He is and how He is willing and able to save you.

Scripture Index for Book 4

1. 1 John 1

2. Matthew 11:25-30
    1 Timothy 1:15

3. Exodus 33:7-11
    Proverbs 17:7; 18:24
    1 Corinthians 15:33
    James 4:4

4. Psalm 50:17; 108:4
    Micah 7:18
    Matthew 10:19
    Luke 21:15
    2 Corinthians 2:13
    Philemon 6

5. Genesis 45:21-28
    Isaiah 65:24
    Luke 18:13; Luke 2:29-30
    2 Corinthians 6:17-18

6. Deuteronomy 6:6-7
    2 Chronicles 7:14
    Jeremiah 29:13
    Joel 1:3
    Mark 11:24
    Luke 18:13; Luke 18:9-14
    James 5:16
    1 John 3:22

7. Ecclesiastes 9:10
    Jeremiah 8:20 & 22
    Matthew 20:6; 20:1-6
    John 9:4

8.   Ecclesiastes 12
         Matthew 9:5
         Luke 18:13

9.   Psalm 66:20
         Matthew 1:21
         John 3:1-21

10.   Joshua 24:14-28
         Isaiah 61:10
         Malachi 3:16-18
         1 John 1:7

11.   Mark 10:28-30

12.   Ephesians 6:5-9
         Hebrews 7:25

13.   Psalm 68:1-10

14.   Ruth 1:15-18
         Psalm 139:7-12
         Jonah 1 & 2

15.   John 15:12-17

16.   Matthew 6:19-21; 19:16-26
         Colossians 3:2

17.   Acts 24:22-27
         2 Corinthians 6:2

18.   Luke 16:19-31

19.   Ephesians 6:13
         Hebrews 13:1-6
         James 4:7

20. James 5:13-15

21. Isaiah 1:16-20
    Luke 15:11-23
    Romans 11:33

22. Isaiah 49:8-13
    Romans 6:23

23. Matthew 7:13-14

24. Psalm 103:10-12
    Isaiah 1:18
    Isaiah 44:21-28
    Micah 7:18-19

25. Matthew 21:12-17

26. Luke 11:5-13

27. Luke 18:15-17

28. 1 Samuel 17:1-58

29. Acts 20:32-38

30. Luke 15:1-7

31. Psalm 18:30
    John 16:15-21

Answers to Questions

1. Forgive us (1 John 1:9).

2. Sinners.

3. With kindness.

4. With a verse from the Bible (Psalm 50:17). The acknowledging of every good thing which is in you in Christ Jesus.

5. The publican's prayer (Luke 18:13).

6. The Pharisee. Teach your children God's Word.

7. He had learned to read Braille at a special school. Discuss.

8. It left his body and went to be with Jesus.

9. He knew that God hears all penitent sinners.

10. By the witness of the Watsons' family worship. Jewels.

11. A hundred times.

12. For discussion or personal application.

13. Friend of the fatherless.

14. God. He caused a great storm so that Jonah had to be thrown into the sea and then saved by a big fish. The opposite.

15. So that He could save sinners from their sins.

16. Because he had no treasure in heaven. Set your affection on things above not on earthly things.

17. We can only be sure of now, not tomorrow. To show John how foolish it was to delay seeking salvation.

18. Poor John, because his treasure was in heaven.

19. Jesus had been kind to them and had told His followers to be like Him.

20. It reminded her of Susan's prayers.

21. The prodigal son. His life had been just like that.

22. The Holy Spirit applied them to his heart.

23. His lifestyle was one which led away from God.

24. He blots them out (Acts 3:19).

25. For personal application.

26. God.

27. Childlike faith (Luke 18:17).

28. For discussion or personal application.

29. No. "It is more blessed to give than to receive" (Acts 20:35).

30. The Good Shepherd.

31. For personal application.

Other books published by Christian
Focus Publications in connection with
Reformation Heritage Books.

*Bible Questions and Answers
for Children* by Carine Mackenzie
and
Teachers' Manual by Diana Kleyn.

ISBN   1-85792-702-8
         1-85792-701-4

Doctrines and subjects covered in
these two titles include:

God

Creation

How man sinned

What happened because of sin

Salvation

Jesus as Prophet, Priest, and King

The Ten Commandments

Keeping God's Laws

The Way to be Saved

Experiencing God's salvation

Baptism and the Lord's Supper

Prayer

Where is Jesus now?

Death

Hell

Heaven

Building on the Rock
Books 1-5

If you enjoyed this book:

Book 4
How God Used a
Drought and an
Umbrella

Faithful Witnesses and
Childhood Faith

You will also enjoy the
others in this series
by Joel R. Beeke
and Diana Kleyn

Book 1
How God Used
a Thunderstorm

Virtuous Living and The Value of Scripture

Book 2
How God Stopped
the Pirates

Missionary Tales and
Remarkable Conversions

Book 3
How God Used
a Snowdrift

Honoring God and
Dramatic Deliverances

Book 5
How God Sent a Dog
to Save a Family

God's Care and
Childhood Faith

Classic Devotions by F.L. Mortimer

Use these books alongside an open Bible and you will learn more about characters such as Cain and Abel, Abraham, Moses, and Joshua, among others. You will enjoy the discussion generated and the time devoted to devotions and getting into God's Word. Investigate the Scriptures and build your knowledge with question and answer sessions with F. L. Mortimer's range of classic material. Written over a hundred years ago, this material has been updated to include activities and discussion starters for today's family.

ISBN: 1-85792-5858
            1-85792-5866
            1-85792-5912

Mary Jones and her Bible

a true life story
a classic favorite

The traditional story of the young Welsh girl who treasured God's Word and struggled for many years to get a copy of her own. An excellent reminder of our Christian heritage. ISBN:1-85792-5688

The Complete Classic Range:
Worth Collecting

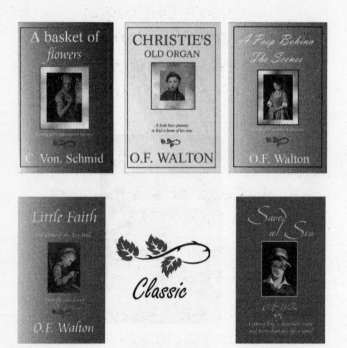

A Basket of Flowers
1-85792-5254

Christie's Old Organ
1-85792-5238

A Peep Behind the Scenes
1-85792-5254

Little Faith
1-85792-567X

Childhood's Years
1-85792-713-3

Saved at Sea
1-85792-795-8

Children's Stories
by D L Moody
1-85792-640-4

Mary Jones and Her Bible
1-85792-5688

Children's Stories by J C Ryle
1-85792-639-0

Fiction books with God's message of truth
Freestyle - 12+
Flamingo - 9- 12
Fulmar - 7-10 years
Check out our webpage for further
details: www.christianfocus.com

TRAIL BLAZERS

Real life stories of people used by God:
George Muller 1-85792-5491
Corrie Ten Boom 1-85792-116-X
Mary Slessor 1-85792-3480
Isobel Kuhn 1-85792-6102
Martyn Lloyd Jones 1-85792-3499
William Wilberforce 1-85792-3715
Richard Wurmbrand 1-85792-2980]
Adoniram Judson 1-85792-6609
Hudson Taylor 1-85792-4231
C S Lewis 1-85792-4878

Bible Stories and Non Fiction

Bible Time, Bible Wise, Bible Alive and The Bible Explorer

All by Carine Mackenzie

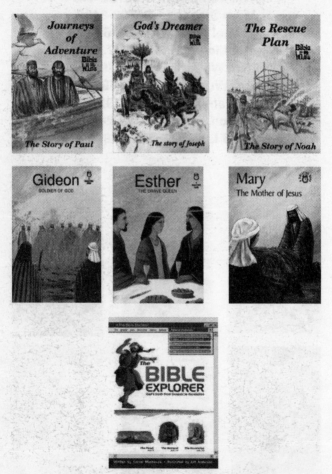

The Bible Explorer: 1857925335

BIBLE ALIVE

1-85792-749-4 Jesus The Child
1-85792-750-8 Jesus The Storyteller
1-85792-751-6 Jesus The Healer
1-85792-752-4 Jesus The Miracle Worker
1-85792-753-2 Jesus The Teacher
1-85792-754-0 Jesus The Saviour

Rainforest Adventures 1857926277
Amazon Adventures 1857924401